SPY KIDS ADVENTURES

FREEZE FRAME

READ ALL THE SPY KIDS™ ADVENTURES!

COMING SOON!

Based on the characters
by Robert Rodriguez

Written by Elizabeth Lenhard

VOLO

HYPERION
MIRAMAX BOOKS
New York

Text copyright © 2004 by Miramax Film Corp.
Spy Kids™ is a trademark and the exclusive property of Miramax Film Corp.
under license from Dimension Films, a division of Miramax Film Corp.
All rights reserved.

For information address Hyperion Paperbacks for Children,
114 Fifth Avenue, New York, New York 10011-5690.

Printed in the United States of America

First Edition

1 3 5 7 9 10 8 6 4 2

This book is set in 13/17 New Baskerville.

ISBN 0-7868-1806-9

Visit www.spykids.com

CHAPTER 1

Carmen Cortez walked into the sunny kitchen of her family home with a sigh of happiness. It was the first day of her winter break from school. She had two whole weeks to just hang out and rela—

Klaaaannnnggg!

"Aaagh!" Carmen cried loudly, clapping her hands over her ears. "What was tha—"

BANG! BANG! Bangbangbangbang!

Cringing in pain, Carmen glanced wildly around the kitchen. She saw her mother standing at the Mexican-tiled counter, chopping veggies for an omelet. Her dad was sipping *café con leche* and reading an important-looking document. But one Cortez family member was missing.

"Is that Juni making all that noise?" Carmen asked her parents over the clatter.

"Juni," Mom confirmed, looking up from her cutting board to shoot her daughter a good-natured grin.

"He's in the workshop," Dad added in his Spanish-accented voice. "Your brother! It's his first day of winter vacation, and he's already hard at work. That's my boy!"

"Working, huh?" Carmen muttered. "Somehow I find that hard to believe." She stomped across the kitchen to the basement stairs. Then she headed down to the workshop to do a little investigating.

Investigation came naturally to Carmen. You see, she was more than just an ordinary twelve-year-old girl. She was also . . . an international superspy!

Carmen was a martial-arts black belt and a master of disguise. She could kick butt in a dozen different languages. Through her work for a top-secret government agency called the OSS, she thwarted evil on a regular basis.

The only thing Carmen *couldn't* do was duck her annoying little brother, Juni. You see, he was a Spy Kid, too. In fact, he was Carmen's partner. Together, the Cortez kids had tamed other bad guys, like the evil entertainer Fegan Floop. They'd beaten the Toymaker at his own sinister computer games and aced many other missions as well.

As spies, Carmen and Juni Cortez were an inseparable team.

But that didn't mean Carmen just had to put up with Juni's shenanigans—not *this* early in the morning! And not without a fight.

As she slunk down the narrow corridor that separated the basement workshop from the basement spy-training room, Carmen glanced down. As usual, she was sporting her OSS uniform—black cargo pants with pockets packed and a tangerine-colored, high-tech, OSS T-shirt. (It was fireproof, bulletproof, *and* pretty.) She was also wearing a utility belt positively dripping with gadgets and gizmos.

"Let's see," she whispered, eyeing her various tools with a sneaky smile. "I could gum him up with the Bazooka Bazooka, but that would be really messy, and then I'd have to clean it up.

"I could out-klang him with my Sooper-Skool-Bell!" she mused, lifting a small but powerful brass bell from its hook. Then she reconsidered. "Nah . . . it lacks subtlety. And as for the Swat 'n' Splat—I don't think Uncle Machete has worked out all its kinks yet."

Uncle Machete was Dad's big brother *and* the greatest gadget inventor the OSS had ever known. But sometimes the final versions of Uncle Machete's gizmos turned out a bit glitchy. The Swat 'n' Splat, for instance, was a giant, virtual flyswatter created to squish villains into submission. The last time Carmen had deployed it, the flyswatter had dissolved into a giant puddle of purple goo!

Shuddering to think of how many paper towels it would take to clean *that* up, Carmen decided to fight Juni the classic way—with good old sisterly bullying!

"Hey!" she yelled, storming into the family workshop. She peered over the giant wooden lathe and through the opening of the hanging quilt frame. Just beyond this equipment, she spotted her brother, crouched on the floor. His cheeks were red from the reflected glow of the fiery blacksmithing furnace *and* from the rigorous hammering he was inflicting upon a vehicle of some kind. The thing was red and shiny. It looked like a cross between a scooter and a sled, with a little bit of airplane thrown in for good measure.

It also looked . . . finished. A moment after Carmen made her angry entrance, Juni stopped hammering. He wiped off his brow with a satisfied sigh.

"What the heck is that thing?" Carmen demanded.

Juni got to his feet and grinned down at the vehicle.

"Carmen," he announced. "I give you the Bob-a-Luuuge."

Juni howled the vehicle's name with the exuberance of a Cuban bandleader. He smiled and added, "It's a brand-new Machete Cortez design—some assembly required."

"Apparently," Carmen noted drily. She wiggled a finger in her still-ringing ear. "So, what *is* a Bob-a-Luuuge?"

"A cross between a bobsled and a luge, of course," Juni scoffed.

"Right. Of course," Carmen sputtered. She walked over to one of the workshop's windows and pointed out at a meadow that was dotted with wildflowers. The sky was blue and cloudless. The sun was blazing. It was the most unwintry winter's day ever.

"Hello?" she said. "In case you haven't noticed, we live in a warm, totally snow-free climate."

"Duh," Juni said. "That's why Uncle Machete included an extra attachment, just for *my* Bob-a-Luuuge."

He reached into a wooden packing crate and pulled out two rubber belts lined with tiny ball bearings. He looped both belts around the Bob-a-Luuuge's blades; then he gave them each a spin.

They whirled around the blades like well-oiled bicycle tires.

"Grass-ready," Juni announced.

"Uh-huh," Carmen said skeptically.

"Hey," her brother shrugged as he hauled the Bob-a-Luuuge out of the workshop. "If you're too chicken to give it a test run, I'll go myself."

"Chicken?!" Carmen screeched. "Listen, turkey. When that Bob-a-Luuuge makes its first ridiculous run, I'm on it!"

"Oh, yeah?" Juni challenged.

"Yeah!"

"Well . . . come on, then," Juni said with another shrug.

The spy sibs walked out the basement door to their backyard. At the end of the flowery meadow, the grass gave way to a rocky cliff, which in turn led down to the ocean. The slope was steep. It was treacherous. It was just the sort of place one would expect the Cortez family to live. You see, Carmen and Juni weren't the only spies in the family. Their parents were in the saving-the-world business, too! From the moment Ingrid and Gregorio Cortez met, they had been all about daring and drama.

Carmen and Juni had heard their parents' story

many times, but they never tired of it. Before Mom and Dad had become, well, Mom and Dad, they had been Ingrid Johanssen and Gregorio Cortez, the most ruthless spies their respective countries had ever produced. They were both so good at their jobs, in fact, that they'd been a danger to each other. So Ingrid's bosses had told her to take Gregorio out. And Gregorio's handlers had told him to take care of Ingrid.

Instead . . . the two spies had fallen in love.

No sooner had they gotten married than yet another enemy attacked, spraying their wedding party with bullets. Though the Cortez couple had suavely parachuted to safety from their cliff-side ceremony, the incident had given them pause. Their death-defying lifestyle was not terribly family-friendly!

So, when the Cortez kids had arrived on the scene, Mom and Dad had decided to drop out of the spy biz. Leading the humdrum lives of ordinary parents, they drove their offspring to school and soccer practice. They served sensible dinners. They worked as computer consultants.

One fateful day, however, the OSS called upon Ingrid and Gregorio for one last, and apparently irresistible, mission. With Carmen and Juni none the wiser, the 'rents had dashed off to save the world.

The only problem? All those years off the job had made Mom and Dad a little rusty. Minutes into their mission, they'd been captured. When Carmen and Juni learned that their parents were in peril, they'd leapt into action, saving their parents' butts and completing their mission.

The whole Cortez family had been spying together ever since.

And now, Carmen and Juni's spy skills were really going to come in handy. They were going to need every ounce of their strength and savvy to navigate the Bob-a-Luuuge down the rocky cliff.

As they walked down the sloping lawn, Juni squared his shoulders.

Carmen set her jaw.

And they *both* worked hard to hide their mounting apprehension.

"Ready?" Juni said.

"Ready!" Carmen replied.

The kids clambered onto the shiny, red sled and pushed off!

"Aiiiiigggggh!" they shrieked, as the sled began to careen down the cliff.

Bonk!

The Bob-a-Luuuge hit a rock and tipped sideways. But somehow, Uncle Machete's ball-bearing belts kept rolling.

"Accckkk!" Carmen and Juni screamed, as their strange sled ran over a rabbit hole.

"Oooooof!" they yelled, as the Bob-a-Luuuge jostled around a juniper tree!

"Aaaaaaaaghhh!" the Spy Kids shrieked. Now the vehicle was launching off a log, becoming altogether airborne!

The Spy Kids screamed some more. They kept on screaming until the Bob-a-Luuuge came to a halt. . . .

The Bob-a-Luuuge stopped at the base of the cliff. Its glossy, red exterior was scraped and splintered, and its passengers were battered and bewildered!

Painfully, they rolled off the sled and crawled to the beach. They flopped onto their backs, breathing hard and blinking into the sunny sky.

"Snowwww," Juni groaned. "If only we had snow."

Carmen shook her fist at the sparkling sky.

"A curse upon our sunny clime!" she yelled.

After a few more minutes of moaning, the Spy Kids noticed that their bumps and bruises had stopped throbbing. Juni pulled himself to his feet and began to fold up the Bob-a-Luuuge.

"Uncle Machete made the sled collapsible, for ease of use," Juni explained when Carmen glanced over.

"Ease of use," she said with a dry laugh. "That's a good one."

She hauled herself to her feet as well, dusting the sand from her clothes and sighing.

"Well, that settles it," she said. "Once again, we're going to spend our winter break yearning for actual winter. Pining for powder. Sighing for snow—"

Ahhhh-WHOOOOP! Ahhhh-WHOOOOP! Ahhhh-WHOOOOP!

High above them, a siren was sounding from their house! And that was no breakfast bell. It was the blaring of the OSS alarm!

"So much for our winter break, *period*!" Juni announced, as he finished snapping the Bob-a-Luuuge into a compact bundle. "It's mission time! Let's head home!"

CHAPTER 2

With no time to lose, the Spy Kids each reached for tiny buttons on their spy watches.

Spy watches, of course, were no ordinary wristwatches. No, they're complex computers, satellite mapping systems, telecommunications hubs, *and* remote-control devices for Carmen and Juni's various other gadgets.

At the moment, the gadgets in question were the kids' rocket shoes! The minute Carmen and Juni pressed their remote ignition buttons, long tongues of flame shot out of the backs of their sneakers. With a loud *fwoooooom*, the kids shot into the air. They flew straight up along the cliff side, then swooped toward home. Juni executed a wild loop-de-loop and landed neatly next to the kitchen door. Carmen skidded to the grass behind him.

"Show-off," she said to her acrobatic brother.

Juni merely cackled with delight, before extinguishing his shoe's rockets.

With their heels still smoking, the Spy Kids rushed through the kitchen door to find their parents—checking out the contents of the freezer?

"Uh," Carmen asked her parents carefully, "is this *really* the right time for a snack?"

"Yeah," Juni echoed. "But, as long as you're in there, do we have any ice-cream sandwiches?"

While Dad gave his son a baleful look, Mom reached deep into the freezer and pulled out a box of frozen pancakes.

"Well . . . I guess pancakes would make a good snack, too," Juni allowed.

Mom hadn't been trying to indulge Juni's sweet tooth. She was actually making way for . . . a computer screen! Attached to a long, robotic arm, the screen shot out of the freezer with a whoosh of icy-cold air. It hovered in front of the spies, crackling as it began to thaw.

Carmen and Juni glanced at each other, eyebrows raised. They'd seen their mother's makeup mirror and the microwave oven transformed into classified computer screens. But *this* was new.

The computer screen suddenly sprang to life. And gazing out of that screen—in a striped ski suit and a pair of cool, amber goggles—was the head of the OSS, Diego Devlin. Taking care not to muss his perfect, Caesar-style haircut, Devlin shifted the goggles to the top of his head. He smiled at the Spy Kids.

"Carmen, Juni," he said. "I know you're just starting your winter vacation. Lots of beach time and frolicking in the sunshine. Ah! What I wouldn't give to live in a balmy climate like yours."

"Uh . . . yeah, it's great, Mr. Devlin," Carmen said politely.

Juni scowled as he eyed a new Bob-a-Luuuge bruise that was sprouting on his arm.

"That's why I feel a little guilty sending you on this next assignment," Devlin continued. "But you *are* the best Spy Kids in the agency. And this is definitely not a job for a grown-up. Especially one with an aversion to snow."

Juni jumped.

"Did you say . . . snow?"

"Great big hills of fresh powder, to be exact," Devlin answered. "Kids, pack your long underwear! We're sending you to the Brockenhip Ski Resort, in blustery Moonshag, Colorado."

"Blustery?" Carmen gasped. "As in, windburned cheeks and chapped lips?"

"Not to mention cold, damp socks and hat hair?" Juni cried.

"Oh, now I feel terrible," Devlin said. "But kids, I must remind you—you are honor-bound as OSS agents to accept this missio—"

"*Yayyyyyy!*" Carmen and Juni blurted out together. They began jumping up and down.

"Skiing!" Juni cried. "Wa-hoo!"

"Snow, snow, snow, and more snow," Carmen shrieked. "It's a dream come true."

"Forgive them, Devlin," Dad said, winking at the computer screen. "Clearly, my own warm-blooded Spanish genes skipped a generation."

"And it looks like their spy instincts might be a bit frozen, too," Mom said. Gently, she nudged her children. "Uh, kids, did you forget that you have a *mission* at this resort? Beyond luxuriating in the chilly weather, that is."

"Oh . . . oh, yeah," Juni said. He and Carmen abruptly stopped jumping up and down.

"Sorry, Mr. Devlin," Carmen said, trying to paste a frown over her giddy grin. "Yes, of course—the mission. Why *are* we snowbound?"

"Well, you'll be going undercover," Devlin began. "Brockenhip has an intensive, children's ski program that starts tomorrow. Call it Winter Camp, if you will. The instructors are the cream of the crop—many of them are Olympic athletes!"

"Oh. My. God," Carmen squeaked under her breath.

"This sounds like the coolest mission ever!" Juni squeaked back.

"While you're posing as skiing students," Devlin continued, "you'll be investigating some funny happenings in Moonshag, the quaint mountain town where Brockenhip is located."

"When you say funny, Mr. Devlin," Juni asked seriously. "Do you mean 'funny ha-ha'?"

"I mean 'funny weird,'" Devlin replied, just as seriously. "A crime wave is sweeping the town. The culprits seem to grow more numerous with each passing day. And all of these evildoers look very fishy—literally. They're pale and cold, with icy, mean eyes."

"What are these baddies doing?" Carmen asked. Her excitement had been replaced by indignation.

"They're committing everything, from acts of petty meanness to serious theft," Devlin answered. "And now, they've begun beating people up! We need to figure out what's up with these cold criminals, before things get any worse. That's why you have to hit the ski lifts, ASAP.

"In the mornings," Devlin continued, "you'll pose as students in the Brockenhip Junior Ski Workshop. But once school's out, you'll hit the town, gathering intel for our crime-fighting cause."

"Sounds like Ingrid and I will be sitting this mission out, then?" Dad asked Devlin hopefully. After all, he *did* like the balmy weather at home.

"Yup," Devlin said. "You should be ready to provide backup, but, for now, this one's all about the offspring."

And so, the next morning found Carmen and Juni Cortez arriving—alone—in Moonshag, Colorado. As a shuttle bus carried the kids from the airport to the Brockenhip resort, Carmen whispered a warning to her brother.

"Remember," she said. "We're not supposed to be seasoned, cynical spies who've seen the worst and lived to tell about it. We're supposed to be starry-eyed young skiers. So act like one."

"What?! You want me to be all dorky?" Juni protested. He made his voice go squeaky and babyish—and sarcastic.

"Oooh!" he yelped. "I'm so excited to see snow! Wow-eee! A real, live, famous Olympic athlete!"

Juni crossed his arms over his stomach and

returned to his normal, slightly less squeaky voice.

"Well, I won't do it," he declared. "Even under-cover, I gotta be me. As in—cool!"

"Uh-huh," Carmen said drily.

"What?!" Juni protested. "I'm cool."

"Not."

"Am too!"

"*Un*cool!"

"Carmen!" Juni bellowed. "You'd better stop calling me names or I'll . . . I'll . . ."

As the shuttle bus skidded to a halt, Juni's voice trailed off. With one look out the van window, he'd lost his train of thought.

As if in a trance, Juni threw open the shuttle bus's door and stumbled out onto a snowy field. He stared at the long swath of craggy mountains lined with ski runs; at the kids tromping through the snow carrying snowboards and skis; at a small, wooden, snack shack, where glamorous-looking athletes were sipping hot chocolate; and at the resort's mammoth lodge, which looked like a sprawling, ten-story log cabin!

Resting near the top of Brockenhip's most dramatic mountain, the lodge had grand turrets and cozy-looking bay windows. The building housed the ski students' dorm, a bustling cafeteria, a game room, and lots of other amenities. It was like a Lincoln-Log dream house!

"Oooooh!" Juni squealed. "Check out the giant log cabin, Carmen! And how 'bout all this snow! So soft and white and . . . snowy! And look at that guy over there! I swear I saw him on TV last week, breaking his personal record. I gotta get his autograph. *And* a hot chocolate. Ooooh! I loooove ski camp!"

Carmen pulled their bags out of the van and tromped over to her brother, rolling her eyes.

"I have two words for you," she said. "Un. Cool."

Juni was about to make a retort when suddenly, Carmen pulled a pretty uncool move herself! She went flying through the air, screeching in alarm, until she landed facedown in the snow with a graceless grunt!

Of course, she hadn't pulled this little stunt voluntarily. It was a kid on a snowboard who had sent her flying. He'd just come out of nowhere and careened into her! Now the punk skidded to a halt, spraying a messy fan of snow all over the Spy Kids as he did. His billowing, lime-green fleece sagged around his skinny torso, and his snow-dusted dreadlocks came to a rest upon his cheeks.

"Heads up, dudes," the snowboarder drawled.

"Same to you," Carmen said. "What's the deal, just plowing into me like tha—"

Swiiiish! Skiiiidddd! Cruuuunch!

Before Carmen could even finish her rant, she and Juni were suddenly surrounded by three *other* scruffy snowboarders. They regarded the Spy Kids with mischievous grins.

"Dude," said one guy in a tall, pointy, fleece cap. He was talking to his dreadlocked friend. "What are you doing, spraying the newbies? Uncool, man."

Then the guy turned to Carmen and Juni and held out a mittened hand for a shake.

"Sorry about my bud here," he said. "He's a bit of a loose cannon."

"Whatever," Carmen muttered. Juni didn't answer. He was too busy ogling the guy's snowboard, which was scuffed and battered and covered with comic-book decals. It was coooool!

"My name's Clark," the guy in the fleece hat said. "My rude friend over there is Brat. And these fellas . . ."

Clark pointed to the other two boarders, who were barely distinguishable from each other in their baggy cargo pants, voluminous fleeces, and lopsided hats.

". . . Are Roddy and Reggie," Clark finished.

"Heeeey," Roddy and Reggie said in unison.

"So," Clark said, eyeing the Spy Kids' long, skinny ski bags. "I see you're skiers?"

"Yeah," Carmen said, sticking her chin out.

"How . . . quaint," Clark responded. "I guess that's why Brat sprayed you. You see, the skiers and boarders have got a little turf war happening on these slopes."

As if to confirm the fact, an adult voice suddenly rang out from a distance.

"I saw you spray those kids," shouted the voice, which was shrill, and thick with a heavy, Italian accent. "You boarders behave yourselves, eh? Or you will deal with me!"

The Spy Kids peered over Clark's shoulder to see a stout man in a tight (make that very tight) skier's unitard. He was bustling over to their group as fast as his plump legs could carry him. When he reached Brat, he unleashed a torrent of anger upon him. That gave Juni the opportunity to nudge Carmen.

"Do you know who that is?" he whispered. "Alfredo Bomba!"

"No!" Carmen gasped. "The famous Italian downhill skier and legendary bad boy?"

"Legendary about ten years ago, anyway," Juni

shrugged. "He was all about living the high life, eating lots of pasta, and going out all night long. But then the next morning he'd casually capture a gold medal. Dad told me about him. He's a big fan."

"I guess the high life catches up with you after a while," Carmen noted, eyeing Bomba's ample paunch and wispy, gray hair.

Of course, that truth might have been lost on Bomba. When he'd finally exhausted his rage at Brat, the boarder, he strode over to the Spy Kids, smiling at them pompously.

"Ah, I hear you whispering," he announced. "It is about me, no? Is true, children. I . . . am Alfredo Bomba. Otherwise know as the slippery noodle."

"Got *that* right," snorted Roddy. (Or was it Reggie?) "The dude *loves* his pasta."

"Slippery noodle," Bomba roared, "refers to my amazing speed on the slopes, you ruffian!"

Then he turned back to Carmen and Juni.

"As I was saying, children, welcome to our workshop. I am the director of the skiing program, passing on to our youth a sport that is a true classic, no? A noble sport of grace and gentlemanly . . ."

Yaaawwwwwwnnn.

The loud, rude noise made Bomba pause. He looked around indignantly for its source. He found it in a lanky woman tromping by. She had scraggly blond braids and sleepy eyes and a snowboard tucked under one arm. In her opposite hand, she held a shiny, green apple.

"Hey," she said, at the tail end of her yawn. "Welcoming some new skiers, Bomba? Just make sure your speech doesn't last so long they miss breakfast! Most important meal 'n all . . ."

The woman took a giant bite out of her apple and made as if to continue to one of the ski runs that began at the edge of the field.

But Bomba wasn't going to let her get away that easily.

"Pokey!" he complained. "Your boarders are plowing down my skiers!"

"Pokey?" Carmen gasped, turning toward the woman excitedly. "As in Pokey Pleat, the champion downhill snowboarder? You're the fastest woman on earth!"

"Un . . . cool," Juni whispered to his starstruck sister.

"Shut . . . up!" she whispered back, as the woman nodded.

"That's me," Pokey Pleat said, with her mouth full of apple. "I'm also the head of the Brockenhip snowboarding program. You should check us out some time. If those skis get, y'know, a little boring."

Pokey turned to face Bomba. "And as for those boarders, they're not *mine*, dude. Snowboarders are a strictly indie crowd. They belong to no one."

Taking another giant bite from her apple, Pokey gazed up at the wintry sky contemplatively. To no one in particular, she added, "But if *I* were a young boarder on my first day of camp, I might chill with the spraying. Seems a little . . . *eager*, if you ask me."

Without another word, Pokey tromped off, leaving a wave of Zen coolness in her wake. Not to mention a couple of red-faced boarders.

"Whatever, dude," Brat said. "Let's get us some Fooglie Puffs and hit the slopes."

The boarders began to amble toward the lodge.

"Fooglie Puffs—the breakfast of champions," Bomba said, scoffing at their skinny backs. "Ha!" Then he stomped plumply away.

Carmen rolled her eyes and began to heave her ski bag onto her shoulder. But Juni stayed where he was, transfixed by the departing snowboarders. Just before the dudes reached the lodge door, he called out to them: "Hey, Clark! Isn't that board a Spew 6000?"

Clark stopped in his tracks and looked back at Juni. He held up his snowboard proudly and said,

"You got that straight. Best board around. How do you know about the Spew 6000, skier?"

"I . . . might have heard about it," Juni said, a bit shyly. "Mind if I take a look?"

Clark tromped back toward Juni, with his buds following behind.

"Take it for a ride," Clark offered. "Let's see if you've got the moxie for the board."

"Yeah?" Juni asked, his eyes lighting up.

"Juni!" Carmen called from the lodge door. "Hello? Remember our mission?"

When the boarders glanced at her quizzically, she hastily added, "As in . . . unpacking and stuff?"

Juni barely heard her. He'd already begun strapping himself into Clark's boots and board. As soon as he was secured to the stubby snowboard, Clark gave him a helpful shove. Juni began to swoosh down the mountainside.

Make that . . . *plummet* down the mountain.

"Aaaaaaghhhh!"

Juni's cries of fear echoed throughout the ski resort!

CHAPTER 3

As the Spy Boy skidded down the mountain, he flailed his arms and wobbled back and forth, screaming his head off all the while. He hadn't felt this loopy since the last time he'd parachuted out of a plane! But at least when he'd jumped into jellyfish-infested waters on a save-the-world mission, he'd known what he was doing! This snowboarding thing, on the other hand, was a complete mystery.

"Whooaa!" Juni yelled as his board slipped out from under his feet. He felt himself go airborne. Then, upside down! Then, miraculously, the board found the snow again, and Juni kept on going!

He swooped to the left.

He veered to the right.

He spun in wild, uncontrollable circles. The snowboard rocked around like a porch glider gone mad.

And then—at last!—Juni landed at the bottom

of the mountain, with a shaky triple spin. He fell into a heap and breathed a sigh of relief.

I made it in one piece, he sighed to himself. And I don't think anyone saw that ridiculous run. My cool rep is intact!

"Dude! Awesome run!"

Urgh, Juni thought miserably. Scratch that. Cringing, he turned to face Brat, who'd yelled the clearly sarcastic remark from the slope directly behind Juni. As soon as Juni turned around, Brat skidded to a halt.

Juni rolled his eyes as a spray of snow covered him from head to toe. Then he braced himself for more mockery. But when he looked up at Brat, he found that the dreadlocked dude's grin looked genuine!

Before Juni could say a word, the rest of the boarders, as well as Carmen, skidded down the slope and joined them. Carmen had tossed on her skis to come to Juni's rescue. Now she skied to a halt in front of him and planted her fists on her hips.

"Juni!" She chastised her brother. "You're such a spaz!"

"Tscha!" Clark said, skidding up to where the group stood. "A *total* spaz!"

Juni felt his windburned cheeks go a shade pinker—until Clark finished his thought.

"You do know, don't you, that in snowboard slang, 'spaz' is the highest form of compliment?" he said. "You're a natural!"

Juni looked around at the other boarders. They were all gazing down at him in admiration!

Feeling his chest fill with pride and relief, Juni clambered to his feet. He used the toe of his boot to flip his snowboard into his hands. Then, he handed it back to Clark and said, "Er . . . of course I knew that. Thanks . . . uh . . . dude!"

"Hey," Clark said to Juni. "Our classes don't start till tomorrow morning. Why don't you borrow one of the lodge's snowboards for the afternoon? You could hang with us and show us the rest of your moves."

"Cool!" Juni crowed.

"Uh . . . Juni," Carmen said through gritted teeth. "A word."

Shrugging at the boarders, Juni tromped over to his sister. She grabbed his elbow and whispered, "Hello? Have you forgotten why we're here? Icy criminals? Reconnaissance? *Spying?!*"

"Forgotten? Not even," Juni retorted under his breath. "I'll spend the afternoon pumping these dudes for information."

"Yeah, right. Between Alley-oops and McTwists," Carmen grumbled.

"We'll see about that," Juni whispered. "Tell ya what. I'll do *my* reconnaissance on the slopes. You do yours in town. And we'll just see who has more intel at day's end."

"Challenge accepted," Carmen said grimly.

The Spy Kids turned their backs on one another and marched off to their separate missions.

Within a couple of hours, Juni had absolutely no intel. But he *had* mastered the Tail Grab, the Misty Flip, and the Inverted Aerial! He'd also learned how to spray an impressive fan of snow at the end of each run, just like Clark and company.

Juni was just getting ready to practice one of those skids when, out of nowhere, a man on a snowboard appeared at the base of his trail. Juni was helpless to stop himself! Before he could change directions, he'd swooshed snow all over the guy and his board.

"Sorry, sir!" Juni cried, hopping off his board and rushing over to dust the snow from the man's fleece.

"Sorry?!" the man blustered. "Sir?! Just who do you think you're talking to? My old man?!"

"Uh . . ."

Juni didn't have a chance to answer. His new buds had just skidded up next to him.

"Hey, Juni doused Manny!" Reggie cried. "Kewwwlll!"

"*Tscha*," the man—Manny—said, slapping Reggie with a high five.

"Uh . . . *you* think that was cool?" Juni asked Manny.

"Dude," Clark explained to Juni. "You're talking to Manny Lass—our boarding teacher at ski camp *and* freestyle boarding champion of the world. Or at least he would be, if he was conventional enough to compete in the Olympics. This guy taught *us* everything we know, from our Alley-oops to our rebel yell."

"DUUUUUDDE!" the boarders all crowed together.

"So you're one of us?" Juni asked Manny after the echo of the rebel yell had subsided.

"Kid," Manny said, shaking his head and running a hand through his shaggy, brown hair. "There's no 'us,' see? We're snowboarders. We're strictly indie."

"That's just what Pokey Pleat told us," Juni said, with a nod.

"Pokey Pleat!" Manny scoffed. "I'd steer clear of

her. She's got an Olympic medal. She's all about training and eating health food. Plus, she's a downhill boarder—all speed and no crazy tricks. She's so mainstream she might as well be . . . a skier."

"Ewww!" Reggie and Roddy said in unison.

"Now, freestylers," Manny said, doing a fancy little spin on his snowboard. "*We* know how to live. We eat for speed. . . ."

Manny pulled a couple of cans of Jitter Cola out of his parka pocket and tossed them to Reggie and Roddy. Then he lobbed a packet of acid-green gummy candy over to Brat.

". . . And we face the mountain without fear," Manny continued. "And if some slowpoke skier gets in our way?"

"Spray 'em," the band of boarders cried en masse. Well, except for Juni. He wasn't about to say it out loud, but harassing skiers didn't seem very sporting to him.

Then again, he thought with a shrug, I'm new to the ways of the board. Maybe after a few more lessons I'll become one with Manny's philosophy. At least I'll learn how to do more of these cool tricks!

As Juni pushed off on his snowboard and began swooping wildly around the slope, he grinned.

"Yup," he said to himself happily. "Boarding's where it's at. I'm totally gonna switch from the ski program to the freestyle one. I can't wait to tell Carmen!"

Carmen drifted down Moonshag's main drag. Behind dark glasses, her eyes scanned the street, scoping out out each sportily dressed passerby. Her hands twitched next to her gadget belt. She was on the ball. She refused to let herself be distracted by souvenir shops. She ignored the enticing scent of fresh fudge, and she averted her eyes from the fabulous, fleecy fashions.

But when she spotted Pokey Pleat across the street, snacking from a bag of trail mix and looking completely cool, Carmen just couldn't resist. She darted to the opposite sidewalk and followed the athlete into a store stocked with expensive ski gear.

As Pokey poked around a display of goggles, Carmen sidled up to her side.

"Hi, Pokey," she said nervously. "I'm Carmen Cortez. We met at the lodge earlier?"

"Oh, yeah," Pokey drawled. "How's it hanging? Gorp?"

Pokey held out her plastic bag of nuts and raisins.

"Thanks!" Carmen said, digging out a handful. "So I *have* to ask you. What did it feel like on that Olympic medal podium?"

"Oh," Pokey said with pensive look. "It felt very . . . uncool!"

"What?" Carmen blurted out in confusion. But then she noticed that Pokey was gazing toward the back of the store. The Spy Girl spun around—just in time to see a pale-skinned, messy-haired dude. He was wearing a baggy fleece jacket and snagging an armful of expensive parkas from a rack!

As he cackled in triumph, another white-faced guy in bright-green cargo pants reached into a glass case and swiped a sports watch!

The dudes gave each other high fives and began to leave the store. But suddenly, the shopkeeper— a slight, elderly man—stepped out from behind a clothing rack and blocked their path.

"Where do you think you're going, you snow-boarding hooligans?" the man demanded.

"Out, grandpa," one of the dudes said.

"Oh, no, you don't," the shopkeeper cried. He clutched at the boarder's arm.

"Oh, yeah, we *do*," the other boarder snapped. He grabbed the man's hand and roughly pulled it from his friend's arm. Then he shoved the shopkeeper to the floor. Unleashing rude guffaws, the boarders then darted from the store.

"Hey!" Carmen cried. She chased after them, dodging around clusters of shoppers and racks of merchandise to get to the shop door. When she finally reached the street, she glanced quickly to her left. And her right. *And* across the street. But she couldn't spot the thieves anywhere. It was as if they'd just melted into the snow!

Kicking at a fallen icicle in frustration, Carmen ran back into the shop. Reaching the doorway, she practically plowed into Pokey, who was on her way out the door.

"You've just seen a robbery," Carmen said to her. "Don't you want to stay and give the police a witness's report?"

Pokey toyed with one of her yellow braids and shrugged.

"Listen, kid," she said. "You can't break a boarder. These guys are renegades. That's their m.o. It's uncool and all, but, hey, it's not hurting me. Besides, I've got a training run in a half hour."

Pokey loped away as Carmen gaped after her.

Talk about indie, she thought in disgust. With citizens like Pokey Pleat, it's a good thing there're spies in town. Speaking of which . . .

Carmen darted across the shop to talk to the store owner. The man was sitting in a chair next to the cash register, surrounded by concerned shoppers. Carmen joined the throng and said, "Are you all right?"

"I'm f—fine," the shopkeeper said. "Just ang—ang—angry, is all. And, suddenly, so c—c—cold!"

Carmen eyed the shopkeeper, a pleasant-looking man who only minutes earlier had been rosy-cheeked and cheerful. Now, his skin was as deathly pale as the thieves' had been. His hands were shaking. And over his chattering teeth, his lips were blue!

Hmmm! Carmen thought. When Devlin said these criminals were cold, he wasn't kidding! It looks like they've given this poor man an icy shot in the arm. This is primo intel. I can't wait to tell Juni!

CHAPTER 4

The next morning, all the Brockenhip students straggled into the cafeteria. Manny and his freestylers sat at a table piled high with boxes of Fooglie Puffs, cups of hot chocolate with marshmallows, psychedelically colored fruit snacks, and burp-inducing sausage patties. Juni joined them with a grin. He rolled up the sleeves of his new, super-baggy, pumpkin-colored fleece, propped his amber goggles up on top of his unruly, red curls, and poured himself a huge bowl of his favorite cereal.

Pokey and her group of energy bar–munching downhill boarders sat at another table. At yet a third, the skiing students ate sensible breakfasts of oatmeal and poached eggs.

At the cafeteria door, Carmen took in the scene and shook her head.

"Talk about a rift," she muttered. Then she shrugged, grabbed some oatmeal, and sat down with the skiers.

As soon as everyone had sat down to breakfast, Alfredo Bomba hauled himself up from the teachers' table, wiping his mouth with a napkin.

"*Attenzione,* young skiers," he cried. "Oh . . . and the rest of you."

"The rest of *who*?" Clark quipped, through a mouthful of sugary puffs. "I don't see anybody here!"

"Right," Manny joked back. "We're the invisible people."

"If only," Pokey Pleat muttered from the next table. "Then the rest of us might get a giant slalom in edgewise."

"As *I* was saying," Bomba interjected, glaring at the two boarding instructors, "I want to welcome all of you to Brockenhip Junior Ski Workshop."

Reggie suddenly unleashed a giant sneeze. A sneeze that sounded a lot like "Ski-LOSERS!"

Shooting another glare at the freestylers' table, Bomba pressed on.

"As you know," he told the campers, "your mornings will be consumed by intensive classes. In the afternoons, you are free to traverse the slopes yourself, or visit the town of Moonshag. Just remember to be back at our lodge by six P.M. for dinner. Lights-out is at ten o'clock."

"That is key," Pokey piped up. "Everyone knows an athlete's peak performance time is between six and ten A.M."

"NERD!" Roddy, Clark, and Brat sneezed together.

Juni couldn't help letting out a snort of laughter, for which he received a scathing glare from his sister over at the skiers' table. Juni stuck his tongue out at her and turned his attention back to Bomba.

"Our Junior Ski Workshops always end with a downhill tournament," Bomba was saying. "This contest features everything from the Super G to the snowboard sprint. However, this year, we're adding a little bonus."

"Oooh, like medals?" Manny blurted out sarcastically. "I've always wanted one of those."

Pokey glared at him but kept her chapped lips clamped shut.

"Like a competition that *counts*," Bomba replied. "For the first time in snowboarding's oh-so-brief history, you surf bums are going to go up against us skiers!"

"What?!" Pokey and Manny cried in unison.

"Ah, at last we have a consensus," Bomba said devilishly. "Yes, the tournament will finish with a battle between skiing and snowboarding. This will be a chance for the world to see which is the better sport. Skiing? Or . . ."

Bomba let out a loud yawn.

". . . *Bored*-ing," he finished.

"That's *boarding*, dude," Brat called out.

"Well, we'll find out, won't we?" Bomba said. "As will all the viewers of KCN, which will broadcast the battle, live!"

"The Kick-the-Can Network?" Carmen gasped to a skier sitting next to her, a pretty blond teenager named Jennifer. "That's the biggest sports channel on TV. Juni is always watching it. Whoa, this is huge."

"Yeah, we better get to work," Jennifer said. "If we dash while the boarders are still celebrating, we can make our first run without any interference."

Carmen eyed the boarders' table. The dudes were indeed whooping it up, pumping their fists and pounding on the table, spilling cereal and hot chocolate everywhere. (Juni, Carmen noted, was at least refraining from outright vandalism. He was merely jumping up and down with glee.)

Carmen rolled her eyes and nodded at Jennifer. She took one last spoonful of oatmeal and followed Alfredo Bomba and the other skiers out to the slopes.

* * *

A half hour later, Juni stood on the lip of Brockenhip's half-pipe, trying to psych himself into executing a McTwist.

He took a deep breath.

And he took another.

And then one more for good measure.

"Bawk, bawk-bawk-bawk," shouted a raspy voice behind him. Juni sighed, then glanced over his fleecy shoulder. Sure enough, Brat was boarding nearby, pointing at Juni and flapping his arms like a chicken.

Oh, the humiliation, Juni thought. How do I get out of this fix?

Swiiish. Swiisssh. Swiiish!

The sound of skiers schussing suddenly filled the air. Brat jumped. He turned his back on Juni and gazed expectantly up the slope. When a pack of neatly dressed, rosy-cheeked skiers suddenly swooped into view, Brat bellowed, "Duuuuuuude!"

He darted after the terrified athletes, harassing them with jeers and snowsprays—completely forgetting about mocking Juni.

I guess *that's* how I get out of it, Juni thought, shaking his head, bewildered about (if grateful for) Brat's obsession with harassing skiers.

Suddenly, Manny alighted next to Juni, doing

a perfect, swooping Tail Grab before he landed.

"Whassup, Juni?"

"What's *down* is more like it," Juni replied, nodding at a point about a hundred feet below them. Sure enough, in Brat's wake, one of the skiers had wiped out. Shaking her fist in annoyance, she was pulling herself out of a thicket of bushes.

"I don't get it, Manny," Juni said. "Boarders. Skiers. Can't we all get along?"

"Not even," Manny said. "Juni, *they* are mainstream. They are uncool. They want to suppress all that's wild and different in the rest of us."

Maybe because we're wild, different, and *obnoxious*, Juni thought.

"And Olympic boarders like Pokey are just as bad," Manny went on. "They're total conformists. Juni—it's up to us freestylers to make sure our sport maintains its edge. Speaking of, check out this move. It's called the Haaken Flip."

With utter fearlessness, Manny suddenly kicked off the half-pipe's lip, swooping down into the icy pit. He skimmed up the opposite side of the depression and became airborne. He twisted, flipped, and loop-de-looped with all the grace of a sunfish. He made a wild landing, pumped his fist, and shot Juni a rakish smile.

Juni was dazzled.

In fact, not since he'd first taken up spying had he been so inspired! He *had* to learn the Haaken Flip. *And* the Phillips 66 and the 720 Spin!

But did that mean he had to adopt Manny's renegade ways?

Juni's shoulders sagged. If he remained a Goody Two-shoes, the other boarders were sure to dis him. But terrorizing bunny hillers and snow-spraying innocent skiers was not very Cortez-like behavior. OSS spies were supposed to stop wars before they'd begun, not start them!

Schussss. Schuussss. Schussss.

Juni glanced morosely at a skier swooping down the slope above him. When he saw that the skier had a mane of wavy black hair trailing out of a familiar red hat, his scowl turned into a grin!

Yes, scaring skiers is definitely wrong, Juni thought with a cackle. Unless that skier is your own sister! *There*'s my solution!

Executing his own reckless Tail Grab, Juni waved at Manny and shot onto the trail. With fierce determination, he began to chase the red-hatted skier.

"Carmen Cortez," he called. "You better look out! There's a snowboarder on your butt! Ha-*ha*!"

CHAPTER 5

Carmen swooped gracefully down the mountain, her back straight, her knees bent and together, her ski poles tucked casually beneath her elbows. She was the picture of the perfect student skier.

Fifty yards behind her, Juni swished wildly and swooshed crazily. He crouched low to his board, his mittened hands skimming the snow, and spraying clumps of the icy stuff everywhere. *He* was the picture of the perfect newbie snowboarder.

Had Juni been *just* a boarder, he would have swooped around his sister in a wide arc, landing just beneath her with an abrupt skid. Carmen would have wiped out satisfactorily, and Juni would have continued down the mountain, cackling and hooting.

But Juni was more than just a snowboarder. He was also a spy! So he intended to give this attack some extra kick!

Waving one arm for balance, Juni used the

other to search the pockets of his baggy snow-boarder's pants. Inside the bulging pouch near his right calf, he found just what he was looking for. It was soft, tomato-red, and doughnut-shaped.

Shaking the garment out, Juni crouched lower on his board. Soon, he caught up to his sister. Schussing at her side, he said, "Hey, Carmen, you look kinda cold!"

"Well, in case you haven't noticed, we're sur-rounded by snow," Carmen said before executing a perfect turn. "We weren't exactly raised to be cold-weather creatures in our sunny hometown."

"That's why I brought you this!" Juni said, toss-ing Carmen the soft, red doughnut. Looping her ski poles around her wrists, Carmen swiped the puffy loop out of the air.

"What is it?" she asked suspiciously.

"A down-filled gator," Juni said. "It's a fleecy ring you wear around your neck. I think that it's the next-best thing to a mug of hot chocolate for warm-ing a skier's soul!"

"Uh, thanks," Carmen said with a shrug. She slipped the gator over her head. As it nestled around her neck, she grinned.

"Man, you're right!" she called happily. "This thing is really warm—AAAAAGHHHHHH!"

Before Carmen could finish her praise, her head pitched forward. The next thing she knew, she was somersaulting down the trail! Carmen's left ski flew off and landed in a pine tree. The right ski skidded into a fellow skier's path, causing *him* to tumble, in a series of somersaults.

Finally, Carmen slid to a halt in a grassy embankment. Red-faced with embarrassment, she tried at least to get to her feet in a cool way—with an agile, reverse handspring. She placed a hand next to each ear, then pushed off the snow. Carmen's feet flew into the air, just as she'd intended. But her neck remained pinned to the snow! After an awkward flailing, Carmen found herself flat on her back in the snow once again.

Carmen twisted. She turned. She even yanked at her own neck with both hands. It was no use. She was pinned like a wrestler on a sweaty mat. As she stared up at the sky in chagrin, her brother suddenly appeared next to her, dousing her with a spray of snow.

"Hee, hee!" Juni squealed. "A *down*-filled gator. Get it? There's nowhere for it to take you but down."

"Oh, I get it, all right!" Carmen said. With renewed annoyance, she gripped the gator. After a struggle, she finally succeeded in ripping it away from her neck. A weighty feather (engineered, of course, by Uncle Machete) popped out of the red doughnut, hitting the snow with a thud. Carmen sprang to her feet.

"And now . . ." she declared to her brother, "*you're* gonna get it!"

"Only if you catch me," Juni laughed. He got ready to push off on his snowboard. "Smell ya later, ski-less wonder."

"I wouldn't speak so soon, 'tude-boy," Carmen said threateningly. "After all, you're not the only one who got some snow-ready gizmos from Uncle Machete!"

Carmen clicked the heels of her heavy, plastic ski boots together with a sharp *thwack*. Instantly, two new skis, with extra-swoopy points and freshly waxed blades, popped out of the soles of her boots.

"Ready or *not*," Carmen said, as Juni's face blanched in fear and wonder, "here I come!"

"Noooooo!" Juni shouted, taking off down the mountain.

"Yes!" Carmen yelled. She grabbed the down-filled neck gator and stuffed it into her pocket. Then she plunged after Juni, tucking her head for extra speed.

Juni screamed again, louder and more shrilly than before. In fact, the shriek was bloodcurdling.

"Okay," Carmen scoffed at her brother's back. "*Now* you're just being melodramatic."

"That wasn't me!" Juni shouted over his shoulder.

"Well, if it wasn't you," Carmen jeered, "someone *else* must be in serious trouble!"

As the weight of Carmen's words sank in to both Spy Kids' heads, they skidded to a halt. For a few minutes—a few *crucial* minutes—they'd totally forgotten they were there on a mission. And now, some innocent victim was paying for it!

Feeling terribly guilty, Carmen searched the mountain for the source of the scream. A moment later, it rang out again.

"Helllpp ussssss! *Please!*"

Juni had been wearing his big goggles on top of his neon-green, fleece hat. Now he pulled them down and fitted them over his eyes. Gazing out over Brockenhip's mountain range, he pushed a button on the goggles' rubbery edge. Suddenly, Juni's view of the ski resort was overlaid with a three-dimensional map on one lens, a zoomable locater on the other.

With the powerful tool, Juni located the screamer in an instant. Far below the Spy Kids, a ski lift had snapped one of its cables! A couple of terrified junior skiers were clinging to a lift chair, which was dangling precariously from the end of the frayed wire. Beneath them, other Brockenhippers were covering their eyes and screaming in fear.

"Let's go!" Juni said, darkly. With their fight forgotten, the Spy Kids began to race down the mountain toward the broken ski lift.

As they approached the dangling lift chair, Juni called out to his partner.

"So what do you say?" he asked. "Spy Maneuver #16-C?"

"The one where we take Huffenpuff Hot Air Pills and float up into the sky?" Carmen asked. "Hello? We're supposed to be undercover. That's *way* too obvious. Plus, it's too cold for the hot air to stay hot very long."

"Okay, well, let's hear *your* idea," Juni responded in frustration.

Carmen bit her lip and frowned in thought. And then, it hit her. The perfect solution . . . *and* the perfect revenge.

"Speaking of cold . . ." Carmen said. She reached into her parka pocket.

"Huh?" Juni said over his shoulder. "Carmen, this is no time to be worrying about a case of the shivers. We're almost there, and we're planless!"

In reply, Carmen merely smirked and said, "See ya later—gator!"

She pulled out the weighty, down-filled gator and threw it over Juni's head.

"Aaaaaghhh!" Juni cried. As the gator settled around his neck, he went head over heels. His snowboard's front tip plunged deep into the powder, and he landed face first in the snow. That caused the board's back end to flip up above Juni's legs. And there, Juni came to a halt, his board angled over his back at a perfect forty-five-degree angle.

Yes, forty-five degrees, Carmen thought with a cackle. That's the perfect launching angle for a ski jump!

She crouched low on her skis and positioned herself behind Juni's upended snowboard. Then she skimmed up the board and went hurtling into the air!

"Hold on, you guys!" she called as she flew toward the dangling skiers. In a few seconds, she'd reached the frayed end of the ski lift cable and grabbed it!

"Whew!" Carmen breathed. "It actually worked!"

She checked out her situation. She was about ten feet below the broken lift chair. Clinging to the footrest of that chair were two terrified little campers—seven-year-old twins named Bitsy and Buffy. Carmen had noticed the girls in the cafeteria that morning. They'd looked really cute in their matching pink ski suits. Now, of course, they were sobbing and wailing and . . . slightly less cute. It looked as though Carmen would have to employ some baby-sitting skills in addition to her spy moves.

"Hi, girlfriends," she called up to the kids cheerfully. "Mind if I hang out here with you?"

"Enough with the jokes!" Bitsy cried. "Get us down from this thing!"

O-kay, getting less cute by the minute, Carmen muttered to herself. I guess there's no time to lose.

She gazed down at the snow beneath her. It looked icy and slick and very far away. The thought of crash-landing on that glassy surface made her cringe.

Re-gripping the broken cable, which was slick with frost, she pushed a button on her spy watch with her nose.

"Juni? Are you there?" she asked through the watch's walkie-talkie.

"Barely," Juni replied through her speaker. "*Ptew, ptew!* I've got a mouth full of snow!"

"Well, if we don't get some cushion for our fall," she retorted, "the girls and I are going to have mouths full of loose teeth! Do something. And fast!"

"Roger," Juni said, more briskly now. "Over and out."

As her spy watch sputtered into silence, Carmen turned to the girls.

"Who's up for a parachute ride?" she asked cheerfully.

"*Waahhhhhhh!*" Bitsy and Buffy screamed.

"Oh, brother," Carmen muttered, rolling her eyes as she inched her way up the cable toward the panicked girls. "Hurry up, Juni!"

Juni lumbered to a standing position on his snowboard and peered up at Carmen. She was slowly moving, hand over hand, up the broken cable toward the two little girls. As she sidled along, she clicked her ski boots together again. Suddenly, fluttery, canvas wings popped out from either side of her ski blades! They were just wide enough to give Carmen some wind as she fell to earth. It'd be a hard landing, but not a bone-breaking one—that is, *if* she were falling alone. With two seven-year-olds in her arms, however, Juni could tell the wings would never be weightless enough. Carmen hadn't been exaggerating about that crash!

"Okay," Juni muttered desperately. "Cushion. Cushion. What to use? Pine boughs?"

Juni eyed the spiky branches of the pine trees that lined the ski run. They looked anything but soft.

"Okay, how 'bout I get everyone to pile up their fleeces," Juni mused under his breath. He eyed the skiers and boarders huddled beneath the broken lift. There were only about forty of them. Their gear would never pile high enough.

"Oh, no!" Juni cried, shaking his fist in frustration. He shook it so hard he sent his board into a wild spin! A big spray of snow flew out from beneath his blade, hitting him square in the face.

"Great," Juni muttered, spitting out another mouthful of slush.

Glancing at the little pile of fluffy snow he'd kicked up, he had a thought.

And his scowl slowly turned into a grin.

"Yeah!" he suddenly cried. "Solution!"

Juni kicked off and began to snowboard in a tight circle just beneath Carmen, Buffy, and Bitsy.

Instantly, Carmen's indignant voice echoed out of his spy watch.

"Juni!" she yelled. "Hello! Rescue time. Save your show-offy Alley-oops for later!"

Juni merely glared up at his sister. He turned his walkie-talkie speaker to OFF.

He skidded around the circle again. And again!

As the onlookers murmured in bewilderment, he picked up speed and kept going around. He was getting so dizzy he thought he might throw up, but he couldn't stop. Every time he looped around the circle, his board kicked up another fluffy drift of snow. The white stuff was piling higher and higher!

In fact, in just a few minutes, Juni had sprayed up a small mountain of it.

Finally, he stopped. Ignoring the queasy feeling in his gut, he looked up at Carmen. By now, she had reached the twins and was positioned between them. Eyeing Juni's homemade snowdrift, she flashed a thumbs-up. Then she grabbed a twin with each arm, and all three girls let go of the cable.

The twins unleashed earsplitting screams as the trio floated downward, barely held aloft by Carmen's winged skis. Just before they really began to speed up, they landed gently upon Juni's pile of fluffy snow.

Completely uninjured, Carmen and the girls skied down the makeshift mountain and skidded to a halt. The sobbing little girls were instantly surrounded by ski camp staffers. Carmen made her way over to her brother.

She grinned and clapped him on the shoulder.

"Well," she announced. "I guess *this* day is officially saved!"

CHAPTER 6

Before Juni could reply, he and his spy sib were surrounded by skiers and boarders alike. The cheering crowd lifted the heroes onto their shoulders and sang their praises. Some even asked for autographs!

Carmen and Juni couldn't help but enjoy the adulation. Eventually the hubbub died down and the revelers skied away. Juni's face grew serious. He pulled off his glove and stuck a hand out toward his sister.

"Sorry about that little gator trick earlier," he said gruffly. "Truce?"

"Truce. And I'm sorry I messed with the gator, too," Carmen replied, giving Juni's hand a shake. "That was some great work. But that doesn't mean our job here is done. We have to—"

"Duuuuuude!"

Juni spun around just in time to fend off the wild snow-sprays of his boarding buds. In true renegade fashion, they'd missed the first celebration. Now they surrounded Juni, whooping, pumping their fists, and pelting him with chocolate bars and other treats.

"That was rad, man," Brat said, shoving past Carmen to pound Juni on the back and thrust a can of Jitter Cola into his hands. Carmen scowled as she stumbled backward.

"Thanks!" Juni said. He popped open the can and took a big slurp.

"Yeah," Clark said, pulling off one of his own gloves. "I never thought of using snow-sprays for, ya know, a good deed before. Put 'er here, dude."

Clark held up his bare hand for a high five. Juni loudly slapped his palm against Clark's. Then he giggled as Reggie and Roddy punched him in the shoulders and sprayed his fleece with more Jitter Cola.

Juni looked up and saw Manny Lass swooshing down the ski run toward him. But Manny *wasn't* pumping his fist or hailing Juni with a triumphant rebel yell. In fact, his stubble-chinned face was drawn into a sour scowl.

Instead, as he skidded to a halt within inches of the group, he said, "How very Boy Scout of you, Juni." He glanced at the sky and mused out loud.

"Huh . . . I guess some people aren't as ready for the indie life as I'd thought."

The other boarders suddenly stopped jumping and hooting. Their smiles faded, along with their exuberant congratulations.

Without a backward glance, Manny kicked off on his board and continued swooshing down the mountain.

"Whoa!" Carmen scoffed from the fringes of the group. "That's about as indie as it gets. Since when is helping someone uncool?"

The snowboarders answered with an uncomfortable silence. They shrugged, busied themselves with clamping their boots back onto their boards, and gave Juni a round of sheepish looks.

"Uh . . . we'll see ya back at the lodge, okay?" Clark said, avoiding Juni's eyes.

"Sure . . ." Juni said hesitantly. "Dude."

En masse, the boarders swooshed after Manny. In a few seconds, Carmen and Juni were alone again.

"Good," Carmen said, shaking her head as she watched the dudes depart. "Now we can talk mission."

Glancing around to make sure nobody else was approaching, she pulled her brother to the edge of the slope. He was still gazing after his buds, sipping pensively at his can of Jitter.

"Like I was saying, Juni," Carmen said breathlessly, "we have to figure out what happened to that ski lift cable. It could have broken by accident, but I don't think so. The ends of the cable were so frosty they were practically blue—just like those guys I saw in town yesterday! Maybe there's a connection between those cold criminals and this incident."

"Maybe," Juni said with a shrug. Loudly, he slurped some more Jitter.

Carmen rolled her eyes. Of all the times for her usually cheery brother to go all moody! She pressed on.

"So let's report this intel to the OSS," she said. "We can go back to the lodge and write up our report while the other kids are doing their afternoon activities. After the agency runs our data though analysis, we can figure out our next step."

Juni looked at his sister with dull eyes. His cheeks had gone a bit pale.

"And while we're at it," Carmen said, "I think you should stop drinking that Jitter stuff. I think all the sugar and caffeine are making you depressed!"

"Know what *I* think?" Juni said sluggishly. "I think you should mind your own beeswax!"

"Juni!" Carmen cried. "Whassup with you?"

The dullness left Juni's eyes. But it was replaced by a cold hardness.

"I should ask you the same question," Juni spat at Carmen. "Last I checked, spying wasn't about reports and waiting for analysis. It was about action. You're just . . . just . . . lame!"

Carmen gasped. In the cool, glam world of the Cortez family, there was no greater insult. She gazed at her brother through a haze of anger and hurt.

Perhaps that's why she didn't notice that Juni's cheeks had suddenly gone a shade paler than before, or that his lips had taken on a blue tinge. All she could see was his betrayal.

So, without another word, she spun on her winged skis and swooshed away.

That night, Carmen hid out in her dorm room. She was sharing the room with a few other girls, but she didn't have to worry about them snooping around in her spy work. *They* were all flirting with boys in the game room or hanging in the cafeteria, snacking on soft-serve ice cream and hot chocolate.

After all, *they* don't have to save the world, Carmen thought sulkily. I wonder if *they* think I'm lame, too!

Morosely, she pulled out her laptop and began typing. First, she wrote up a report of all the intel she'd gathered since arriving at Brockenhip. She found a secured e-mail line and sent it in to the OSS database.

A short while later, she checked her own e-mail account. Of course, there was a loving note from her parents in her in-box. It was addressed to both Spy Kids.

Dear Carmen and Juni, the message read. *The OSS routed your report to us only minutes ago. It looks like you've gathered lots of intel* and *saved two young children. Excellent teamwork, children. We're so proud of you.*

"Teamwork," Carmen muttered to herself. "Ha! If they only knew . . ."

Carmen bit her lip and read on.

We'll begin analysis of your data ASAP. Meanwhile, we hope you find a little time to have fun amidst all your spy work.

"You don't have to tell Juni twice," Carmen complained out loud.

We miss you terribly, the e-mail said in closing. *Save the world soon so you can come home! ;-)*

Much love,

Mom and Dad

Logging off, Carmen toyed with the idea of just

going to bed. But then she punched her pillow and shook her head.

Going to bed early is lame, too, she thought. I'm going down to the game room!

With that, she flounced out of her room and walked through the dorm's sumptuous, log-lined corridor. She descended the grand staircase, which was lined with old-fashioned, wooden skis, skiing trophies, and antique, black-and-white photos of skiers in fur jackets and sheepskin hats. On the fringes of this tableau someone had tacked up a few color snapshots of snowboarders doing aerials and Alley-oops. But there was no other evidence of boarders on the wall of glory.

Carmen sniffed at the snapshots and headed through the lodge's foyer to the game room. When she arrived, it was bustling with activity.

Make that *activities.*

The junior skiers were sitting around a table in the corner, playing chess and backgammon.

In other corner, the downhill boarders had set up a mat where they were having a sit-ups competition.

And over by the video games, the freestyle boarders were yukking it up. Brat was messing with the Ms. Pac-Man game, using a cheat code to fill in the high-score record for the game with his initials.

Reggie and Roddy were whacking their way through a noisy game of air hockey.

And Clark and Juni? Well, they were chewing giant wads of purple gum, then blowing bubbles bigger than their heads. When Juni's bubble exploded all over his face, he merely giggled.

"Kewl," he growled, scraping the gum off his face. "But you know what would be even cooler?"

"What?" Clark said, gnawing on his gum noisily.

"A little game I like to call Stick It to Me," Juni said.

Carmen raised an eyebrow. *This* was new.

"Sounds dorky," Clark scoffed. He raised an eyebrow himself. "But just to humor you, I'll let you explain the rules."

"It's simple, really," Juni said. "I spit. And you predict."

Juni moved his gum to the front of his mouth. Then he threw his head back and . . .

Ptoooooey!

All conversation in the game room suddenly stopped. Skiers and boarders alike watched in awe as the spit-soaked purple wad of gum soared through the air. As it headed for a landing, Clark suddenly yelled, "The TV! It's gonna hit the TV!"

Sure enough, a moment later, the gob landed

smack in the middle of the TV screen. A couple of downhillers who'd been watching a desert-island reality show yowled in protest.

"Cool!" Clark said, with a giant guffaw.

Smiling smugly, Juni walked to the TV and plucked his bubble gum off the screen (leaving a sticky smear behind). He popped the wad back into his mouth.

"Care for another try?" he asked Clark, who nodded eagerly.

Juni chewed. Then he unleashed the wad with another huge *ptoooey*. Carmen's lip curled. This was disgusting! When she heard Clark yell, "The hair of that kid napping on the couch!" she decided she could take no more. Rolling her eyes, she stormed out of the game room.

This has gone beyond being obnoxious, she thought. Now the boarders are being just plain mean. And my brother is the worst offender! I can't believe it!

Feeling a combination of righteous anger and pained confusion, Carmen stomped off to bed.

CHAPTER 7

The next morning in the cafeteria, Carmen wasn't surprised to see her brother pouring a river of chocolate milk onto a giant pile of Fooglie Puffs. He clearly hadn't combed his crazy curls or washed his face that morning. His cheeks were still sticky with remnants of bubble gum.

Carmen sighed. She started to stride over to the oatmeal station without a second glance at her brother. But . . . well, there was just one little problem. As much as Carmen thought Juni was being a big jerk, he was also her little brother, so she couldn't *help* taking a second glance at him. When she did, she realized that, aside from his appalling grooming, Juni wasn't looking so hot.

In fact he looked downright cold.

His fingers were trembling as they clutched his spoonful of Fooglie Puffs. And no matter how much hot chocolate he drank, his cheeks remained pale. Even his lips were a little blue.

Carmen frowned as she arrived at the oatmeal station. As she spooned a big glop of the porridge into her bowl, she looked over her shoulder and gave Juni one more fishy glance. He was still shivering, still surly, and still blue-lipped.

I can't believe it took me this long to realize what's happened to Juni! she thought in shock. Still grasping the gloppy oatmeal spoon in one hand, she thought back to the incident in Moonshag two days earlier. After the robbery, the cheerful shopkeeper had suddenly gone pale, blue-lipped, and shivery.

Carmen searched her photographic memory, replaying the scene. She recalled the shopkeeper's face flushing red with anger as he'd grabbed the thief. The baddie's bud had clutched at the man's hand, yanking it away. Then, he'd shoved the man to the ground. Finally, the boarders had high-fived each other and dashed off.

Carmen homed in on that high five. That slap, she realized, was as essential to snowboarders' body language as was chugging Jitter Cola or kicking up their boards for a Tail Grab. The high five was their hello, their good-bye, their all-purpose aloha.

It was *also* their form of congratulation. For example, Clark had high-fived Juni right after the ski lift save. Very soon after that moment, Juni had turned mean.

And sarcastic.

And shivery!

Carmen plopped the oatmeal spoon back into the porridge vat and spun on her heel. Scowling with determination, she marched toward the snowboarders' table. When she arrived, she was greeted, of course, with a heaping helping of scorn.

"Good morning, Miss Goody Ski Boots," Brat quipped, to the snorts and giggles of his comrades. "Where are your bran flakes?"

"I think I see one hanging out of your nose!" Carmen retorted, glaring at Brat. "Oh, never mind. I must have been mistaken. Bran flakes aren't green."

As Brat's buds guffawed, Carmen turned her attention to Juni. Grabbing his fleecy arm—being careful not to touch his bare hand—she yanked him off his chair.

"Now, if you'll excuse him," Carmen said to the still-sputtering boarders, "I've gotta borrow my brother for a minute."

"What's the dealio . . . *skier*?" Juni demanded as

Carmen began to drag him across the cafeteria floor.

"The *dealio*," Carmen muttered under her breath, "is that if you don't come with me, I'm gonna tell those boarders about your little wart problem!"

Juni's ghostly face grew pale. You see, before Juni became a spy, he'd been a total scaredy-cat. From school bullies to spelling tests, life had frightened him so much his palms had been permanently sweaty. All that sweat had led to warts—one per finger. He'd spent much of the fourth grade covering his hands with Band-Aids and hanging his head in shame. Of course, once he'd begun saving the world on a regular basis, Juni had grown more confident. His warts had become a distant memory—one that he wanted to keep as distant as possible!

So, he nodded sullenly and followed Carmen out of the cafeteria. She led him to the game room and peered around to make sure they were alone. Then she announced to her brother, "Your so-called buds are giving you the big freeze, bro."

"Come again?" Juni said, his voice dripping with 'tude. "*Some* of us here speak, y'know, English?"

Carmen closed her eyes and counted to ten. She couldn't believe her obnoxious little brother could have become so much *more* obnoxious. Taking a deep breath, she tried again.

"You know all those high fives the boarders do?" Carmen said.

"Mmmm . . ." Juni grunted rudely.

"Well, I think those slaps have been passing along some sort of coldness," Carmen continued. "Victims are frozen from the outside in. They get blue and shivery and mean! And I think they've done it to you, Juni!"

Juni snorted. He sneered. Then he spat, "They did not!"

"Did too!" Carmen protested.

"No way!"

"Yes, way!"

"You lie," Juni blurted out.

"I do not—" Carmen huffed in frustration. "Oh, forget it. This is useless. Y'know what? I'm going to handle this like a spy."

"Meaning?" Juni taunted.

"Watch and learn, rudenik," Carmen stated. Before Juni could react, she reached into the pocket of her ski vest and pulled out a handful of foil packets. They had been another pre-skiing gift from Uncle Machete.

"They're hand and foot warmers," her uncle

had told her over the phone after the express package had arrived at the Cortez home. "Just give 'em a squeeze or a step and my secret ingredients will be activated. Your tootsies will be toasty in no time."

"What's in it?" Carmen had asked, giggling as her burly, gruff uncle said "tootsies."

"Ten different kinds of chili pepper, firefly thoraxes, a little mayonnaise," Uncle Machete had said. "You know, the usual . . ."

"O-kay," Carmen had said delicately. She'd been thinking, Gross! I'm *so* not squeezing those things. What if they burst open?

Carmen smiled to herself. Her training had taught her that you never knew when some new gadget might come in handy—even a gross one. So in the end, Carmen had tossed them into her gizmo stash, just in case. Now, she was superglad she had.

She glanced furtively at the label on one of the packets. *Hot Sauce, created by Machete Cortez,* it read. *Squeeze packet gently to attain instant warmth. Use no more than one per hour. This stuff is really hot!*

Perrrrfect, Carmen thought, a scheming glint in her eye. Using a lightning-fast windup, Carmen pelted Juni with one of the packets. It hit, stuck for a moment to his gum-sticky cheek, then fell to the ground.

On Juni's face, however, it left a rectangular-shaped pink spot! The Hot Sauce had begun to warm Juni up!

Carmen threw another packet at him.

"Hey!" Juni scowled as the packet hit him on the neck—leaving another pink rectangle. Juni scooped the Hot Sauce envelope off the floor and whipped it back at Carmen. The warm foil stung as it ricocheted off her arm.

"That does it!" Carmen exclaimed. She tore one of the packets open and launched herself at her brother. Before he could fend her off, Carmen had squirted him with a small geyser of Hot Sauce. The bright-pink goop was gritty with chili powder and lumpy with bug parts. It was dis-*gusting*!

But it was also effective! Even through the goop, Carmen could see Juni's skin becoming bright pink.

Juni shouted in rage and desperately tried to flick the Hot Sauce off his face. But the more he flicked, the more he rubbed the stuff into his skin. And the more the Hot Sauce seeped into his pores, the softer Juni's roars became. By the time his face was wiped clean, his cheeks were flaming with both heat and good cheer. He even had a goofy grin on his face.

Carmen knew Juni was cured completely when he shook his head blearily and said, "Cool goo! What is it?"

Carmen sighed with relief and explained to her confused brother what she thought was behind his bad behavior. When she'd finished, Juni nodded sadly.

"You've gotta be right," he moaned. "The boarders are baddies!"

"So . . . are you going to help me take them down?" Carmen asked apprehensively.

Juni nodded again. He gave Carmen a sheepish glance.

"And, uh," he added, "sorry for the 'tude back there."

"Dude, you were under the influence," Carmen said. "Don't sweat it. Get it?!"

"Hardy-har," Juni said. He dug into one of the pockets of his cargo pants and pulled out a handful of thick rubber bands equipped with buckles.

"Easy-to-pack, elastic handcuffs," he explained, handing Carmen a couple. "Let's get this over with."

Carmen and Juni headed to the cafeteria, determined to make quick, orderly, and professional arrests. But when they arrived, they were chagrined to see that the boarders had already bailed, leaving a trail of candy wrappers and crushed Fooglie Puffs in their wake.

Exchanging worried glances, the kids grabbed Carmen's skis and Juni's board from the rack near the lodge door. They hurried outside, reaching the field in front of the lodge just in time to see their prey clicking their boots onto their snowboards. The guys had chosen to start the day on a treacherous, little-traveled trail on the back of the mountain.

"Dudes!" Juni called.

"Juni, man!" Clark called. "C'mon! There was a good freeze last night. This run is, like, lethal! Pure ice."

"Interesting choice of words," Carmen said, cocking one eyebrow at Clark.

"Watchoo talking about, skier?" the boy sneered.

"Sorry, Clark," Juni said, stepping forward with a pair of the elastic handcuffs at the ready. "By the order of the OSS, we're putting you under arrest."

"Dude?" Clark said in bewilderment.

"Dude!" Brat said in disgust.

Roddy and Reggie didn't say anything at all. They merely exchanged mischievous glances and reached down to tap their snowboards with their mittens. They must have hit hidden ignition buttons, because, suddenly, their boards' tails spouted flames!

An instant later, Clark and Brat jump-started their boards, too.

Before Carmen and Juni had a chance to react, the dudes' snowboards lifted clear off the snow. With a round of smug cackles, the frozen-hearted boarders flew away!

CHAPTER 8

Carmen and Juni looked at each other in shock. This was definitely going to be harder than they'd thought.

"We've gotta catch 'em!" Juni cried. "If only we were wearing *our* rocket shoes."

"We may not have those," Carmen said with fire in her eyes. "But we do have our wits, which is more than those boarding bohunks can say. C'mon, let's do a gadget survey."

The Spy Kids darted behind a pine tree and began digging gizmos out of the pockets of their parkas, cargo pants, and vests. Juni even popped his personal robot, R.A.L.P.H., out from beneath his fleecy hat.

"Subtle, Juni," Carmen said as the mechanical bug skittered cheerfully down Juni's arm.

"R.A.L.P.H. gets lonely if I just leave him in the dorm all day," Juni said. "Besides, he *was* under-cover—literally!"

Juni spun his hat on his finger and stuck his tongue out at his sister.

"Whatever," Carmen said, before frowning at their array of gadgets. She pawed through a Laser Net Deployer, an acid crayon, some Sproinging Soles, and a box of Chameleocandy: all brilliant gizmos, but none of them quite right.

Juni's gadgets, meanwhile, had the obnoxious influence of the boarders written all over them. He had cherry bombs and a couple of whoopee cushions, not to mention a big can of Slip 'n' Slide axle grease, for tripping skiers up in the cafeteria.

"Whoa," Juni breathed. "I really lost my head there, didn't I? Not to mention my spy instincts."

Remorsefully, Juni began to gather his practical-joke devices into a pile to throw away. But suddenly, Carmen grabbed Juni's arm.

"Don't trash those treasures!" she yelped.

"Huh?"

Carmen didn't have time to explain. She grabbed one of Juni's flattened, red whoopee cushions. Then she pawed through her own gadget stash and fished out a couple of wrinkly, pink balls.

"Ewww!" Juni cried. "What are those?"

"Prototypes of the Second Brain," Carmen said. "Dad made them in the OSS lab a long time ago. They're pretty primitive—practically worthless."

"So?" Juni said impatiently. "Why are you wasting time playing with them?"

"Maybe you didn't hear me," Carmen retorted. "I said the Second Brain was *practically* worthless. It does have one great quality—it's an endless automator. It can turn any static object into a mechanical one. And it never runs out of juice. Watch this. . . ."

Carmen attached a Second Brain to one of the whoopee cushions with a small clamp. Instantly, the cushion began inflating and deflating, all on its own! The mountaintop's crisp, morning air was suddenly filled with the sound of flatulence.

"Hee-hee!" Juni giggled.

"No laughing," Carmen grumbled. "Let's try and get through this with a tiny bit of dignity, please! Now, we're gonna need another snowboard."

"I'll handle it," Juni said. Grabbing the bag of cherry bombs, he dashed off.

Meanwhile, Carmen grabbed Juni's board and took several pieces of bubble gum from his gadget pile. She shoved the handful of candy into her mouth. By the time Juni returned, carrying a snowboard beneath his arm, Carmen had chewed the gum until it was good and sticky. Then, she'd used it to affix the ever-flatulent whoopee cushion to the end of Juni's board.

"One whoopee cushion isn't enough to lift me off the ground!" Juni complained.

"Please, let me finish," Carmen said, pulling a small rod from her own gadget arsenal.

"Of course!" Juni said, slapping his forehead. "Uncle Machete's SuperMax battery. It'll turn anything into a powerhouse."

He handed Carmen the new snowboard.

"I traded the cherry bombs for it," he explained. "But the kid says it's gotta be back by noon."

"No problemo," Carmen muttered as she rigged up her own board with a Second Brain, a wad of gum, and her own whoopee cushion.

The Spy Kids latched their boots onto their boards. Then each took a SuperMax battery and (using more of that handy bubble gum) stuck them to their whoopee cushions.

Within seconds, the cushions' gentle *pffft-pffft-pffft*s turned into the loudest, most obnoxious farts ever!

"*Whaaaa, haa, haa!*" Juni roared, collapsing in a fit of giggles.

"No laughing!" Carmen demanded, becoming red in the face. "We've got criminals to catch."

That sobered Juni up quickly. As his grin changed into a determined scowl, he kicked off the snow. His board became airborne on the strength of those powerful *pffffft*s. Then Carmen launched her own board, and they were off!

As Juni surfed through the air, dodging pine trees and scanning the mountain for the runaway boarders, he found that "air-boarding" was just like snowboarding—but even more fun!

Those similarities were of no help to Carmen, though. She'd never been on a board in her life.

"Whaaaaaaa!" she screamed, as her legs tipped to the left and her torso dipped to the right.

"Eeeeeek!" she cried, as her board's tail suddenly flipped over her head.

"Bwwwaaaaaah!" she bellowed, as she was thrown upside down.

"Nice inverted aerial," Juni yelled as he skimmed past his sister. "But shouldn't we be searching for our criminals instead of honing our tricks?"

"Hello?" Carmen cried, finally wobbling back into an upright position. "You think I *meant* to do that? I have a whole new respect for snowboarders!"

"Well, *some* of them," Juni added in alarm. He

pointed to a spot high above them. Carmen followed his gaze and gasped.

Juni had spotted the band of runaway boarders. They were whizzing up the side of the mountain.

"After them!" Carmen said.

PFFFTTT! PFFFFTTT! PFFFFTTT!

With the help of their superpowered whoopee cushions, the Spy Kids skimmed up the cliff side. In seconds, they'd caught up to the snowboarders.

Unfortunately, the tremendous noise made by the Spy Kids' boards gave the dudes plenty of warning. The baddies scattered, laughing uproariously. The Spy Kids went red in the face. But a true spy remembers his or her mission, even in the face of utter humiliation. So Carmen cringed quickly, then recovered her composure.

"I'll take Reggie and Roddy," she said to her brother. "You go for Clark and Brat."

Carmen crouched low on her board to zoom after her targets. As usual, Reggie and Roddy were boarding side by side, smirking and guffawing at each other's wild tricks.

"Perfect . . ." Carmen muttered. She reached into her pocket and pulled out her Laser Net Deployer. She did a quick mental calculation, factoring in her miles per hour, her target distance, and several other crucial factors. At precisely the correct moment, she pushed a button on the small, black rod.

A bright green web of lasers popped out of a tiny hole in the end of the rod. Carmen had timed her deployment so that the net would land directly in front of the speeding boys, snagging them in the air, before they had a chance to veer away.

And the capture definitely would have worked, *if* Carmen's snowboard hadn't suddenly caught an air pocket and tipped sideways at the precise moment she unleashed the Laser Net!

But that's exactly what *did* happen. The glowing green web flew through the air, missing Reggie and Roddy by several feet.

Carmen lost her balance completely and crashed to the ground with a grunt. To add insult to injury, the Laser Net fell onto her own head! After a struggle, she clawed the net away from her face and watched in fury as Reggie and Roddy disappeared into the woods.

A few minutes later, Carmen spotted Juni snowboarding—as opposed to air-boarding—toward her through the woods. His face was dark with anger, and his whoopee cushion—popped and useless—flapped from his board's tail.

Needless to say, Juni was captiveless, too. He dismounted his board and slumped onto the snow next to Carmen.

"Don't ask me why," he said. "But I trusted Clark. He challenged me to an Alley-oop contest. He promised that if he lost, he'd come with me quietly. I thought I had it made. I've got the Alley-oop down cold. Sure enough, I totally won."

"And Clark dashed?" Carmen asked quietly.

"Uh-huh," Juni moaned. "Right after Brat used a blow-dart to pop my whoopee cushion. There was no catching those dudes."

"They're seasoned snowboarders," Carmen pointed out to her brother dejectedly. "There's no way we're going to beat them at their own game."

"So," Juni said, jumping to his feet, "we're going to start playing the game our way. The spy way!"

"Are you thinking what I'm thinking?" Carmen asked, feeling her face brighten as she got to her feet.

"Yup!" her brother replied. He was already dialing a number into the satellite-phone component of his spy watch. "It's time to call in the troops!"

CHAPTER 9

The next morning, Carmen and Juni tromped out to the ski slope, gazing around warily. They were sleep-deprived and bleary-eyed. After all, Carmen had stayed awake in the lodge lobby, watching for the snowboarders' return until two A.M. Juni had taken the early, early, morning shift.

But the boarders had never shown up.

"That's okay," Juni muttered to his sister. "They won't be able to resist Manny's class this morning. He's their idol. They'll be here soon."

As all the student skiers and boarders began to divide into groups and swoosh away with their instructors, the Spy Kids poised for action. They had all sorts of snowboarder-snagging gizmos hidden beneath their puffy parkas—and they were ready to use them!

They watched.

They waited.

And they waited some more.

In a few minutes, all of the Brockenhippers had dispersed, and Carmen and Juni were left alone, dumbstruck. Not only had Clark, Brat, Reggie, and Roddy all bailed, but Manny was AWOL, too!

"This just proves what I suspected," Carmen declared when she found her voice. "Manny Lass is one bad dude! In fact, I bet he's the leader of this soul-freezing gang."

"It sure looks that way," Juni agreed glumly. He couldn't believe he'd been so duped by Manny's coolness.

"I bet this has everything do to with Manny's whole rebel thing," Carmen scoffed loudly. "Snowboarding's going mainstream, so he had to find another way to rebel—by building up an army of icy minions!"

Before Juni could answer, a couple of cross-country skiers came into view. The Spy Kids kept quiet so the outsiders wouldn't overhear their strictly classified chat.

Of course, the skiers had no such worries. The Spy Kids easily overheard their conversation. And the news was *not* good.

"Did you hear? More crazy stuff happened in Moonshag last night," one skier said to the other.

"No, really?"

"Yeah," the first skier continued. "I heard that a guy in cargo pants and a superbaggy fleece . . ."

"Snowboarder," the second skier noted.

"Totally," her companion agreed. "Anyway, he robbed the bank—using a ski pole as a weapon! And as he was running out, he plowed down this guy on crutches. The poor guy had broken his leg on the slopes. Now his other ankle's sprained, too!"

"That's terrible!" the second skier said. "But guess what? *I* heard someone also jerry-rigged every dryer in the Brockenhip Beauty Stop to operate on full blast only. Now there are all these society skiers walking around town with unintended dreadlocks. They're devastated!"

"No!" the first skier cried. "That's, like, cruel and inhumane! Snowboarders are just plain bad."

"Tell me about it. . . ."

The skiers swooshed out of Carmen's and Juni's earshot. When they spoke again, their voices were low and grave.

"Things are getting worse," Carmen said. "The boarders are on a total crime binge!"

"Not *all* boarders," Juni pointed out. "Just those with ice in their veins. But *everyone* in the group is getting the bad rap."

"What's your point?" Carmen said.

"I'm saying that it's not just the citizens of Brockenhip who are in danger," Juni cried. "It's the entire sport of snowboarding! If these thugs go much further, boarders could be banned from every slope in the world. They'll rebel themselves right out of existence!"

"Dude," Carmen said gravely. "The big picture is looking mighty sinister."

"We've gotta do something," Juni declared. "Now!"

Carmen was about to agree when a sound distracted her. She cocked her head to listen harder.

"Sounds like applause," she said of the distant roar.

"And cheers," Juni added, a smile tugging at the corners of his mouth.

"And general expressions of amazement," Carmen said, grinning outright.

"Looks like the troops have arrived!" Juni cried. He hopped onto his snowboard and began swooshing eagerly toward the noise. Carmen followed on her skis.

Halfway down the mountain, the Spy Kids saw that a crowd had gathered. The impromptu audience were gazing, awestruck, at a single skier.

She was clad in a shimmery, silver unitard and the very latest in gear.

She was very beautiful, from her auburn curls to her smiling, green eyes.

And she was putting on an incredible ski ballet show. She spun in graceful circles, executed swanlike flips, and danced across the snow as if she were absolutely weightless.

Among the admirers cheering on the mystery woman was a skier with dark, wavy hair and a pencil-thin mustache.

He spotted the Spy Kids and walked over.

"Ah, you look like discerning junior athletes," the man said to Carmen and Juni. "Surely you recognize the star in our midst?"

"Well, she does look *awfully* familiar," Carmen replied with a twinkle in her eyes. "What's her name?"

The man had a twinkle in his own eyes, which happened to be the exact same shade of brown as Carmen's.

"That, children, is Signe Schuss," the man said. "She is an international ski ballet champion and a member of one of the oldest, wealthiest families in Switzerland. As you can, no doubt, tell from my accent, *I* am a native of Madrid. My name is Don Coyote—Signe's coach."

Don leaned over and whispered to the Spy Kids, "Otherwise known as your loving papa, going undercover with Mom! How are we doing so far?"

"Excellent, Dad," Carmen replied with a grin. "We'll give you your hello-hugs later. In the meantime, keep up the whole aristocratic skier ruse! It's perfect. To those antiestablishment snowboarders, it'll be like Swiss cheese to a rat. I bet you they show their grubby faces within the hour!"

An hour later, "Signe" was still doggedly hotdogging on her balletic skis, and "Don" was still shouting fawning instructions to her from the sidelines. He was also taking faux cell phone calls from Signe's stockbroker and personal fashion stylist.

But the snowboarders still hadn't taken the bait!

Finally, Mom skied over to her husband and children as they stood on the ski slope's edge.

"I am through entertaining all of you!" she said loudly, and in a very convincing "Swiss" accent. "I want to be alone. Don, schedule me a manicure and massage for this afternoon! Children! Out of my way. I will descend the mountain one last time before I retire to my luxurious suite."

As she made her announcement, Mom winked at her kids. With one more glance at the trees scanning for the scruffy snowboarders, Mom gave her family an apologetic shrug and pushed off. In a moment, she'd swooshed around a curve in the trail and ducked out of sight.

"Eh . . . that is too bad," Dad said to Carmen and Juni out of the side of his mouth. (After all, they were supposed to be strangers, so they didn't want anyone to see them talking.) "But don't you worry, *mis niños*. We will get those baddies soon . . . enough?"

Dad's voice trailed off. He cocked his head, listening hard. From farther down the mountain came a chorus of hoots and hollers.

"Do you hear that?" Dad asked Carmen and Juni. "It sounds like—"

"—The war whoops—" Carmen interjected.

"—Of snowboarders!" Juni finished. "Let's go!"

The three Cortezes shot off down the slope. And after only a few twists and turns in the trail, they spotted a scene that made their blood run cold.

Mom was backed up against a snowbank. She was surrounded by a pack of jeering boarders—at least ten of them! Among the throng, Carmen and Juni spotted Clark, Brat, Reggie, Roddy, and . . . Manny!

Everyone in the group looked pale, surly . . . and

shaky. But they weren't too jittery to kick up some snow. They were showering Mom with snow-sprays, doing disorienting flips over her head, ripping her expensive ski parka, and pelting her with Pop Rocks!

"Hey!" Juni shouted as the spies schussed toward the scene. "Knock it off!"

"Or we'll *make* you knock it off," Carmen threatened. The boarders, of course, ignored the Spy Kids. So Carmen and Juni glanced at their father to see what he'd say.

Dad remained silent. But his face was scarier than any taunt he could have uttered. Nobody, but *nobody*, harassed the wife of Gregorio Cortez and got away with it!

Carmen nodded her head determinedly. "Let's move in!" she yelled.

CHAPTER 10

As Dad, Carmen, and Juni banded together to face the band of renegade boarders, Carmen offered a strategy.

"Spy Maneuver #2-D," she declared.

"The Dozen-Egg Scramble?" Juni protested. "Are you sure we shouldn't try, say, The Pinball, or . . . how about my personal favorite, Spy Maneuver #24-J, the Licorice Twist?"

"If you could get your mind off *candy* for one second . . ." Carmen said.

"Children!" Dad roared. "There is no time for bickering. Carmen's right, Junito. The Dozen-Egg Scramble is the perfect approach for this capture."

"Oh . . . all right," Juni said. "Just as long as I don't have to be the whi—"

"You're the whisk," Carmen ordered. "Dad and I will do spatula duty."

"*Awwww!*"

Juni had time to grumble, but there was *no* time

for negotiation. The Cortezes had just skidded up to the scene. Not that the evil snowboarders noticed. They continued to batter Mom with snow-sprays, candy, and jeers.

With a sigh of resignation, Juni twisted his arms around his body. Then he twisted his torso until he was looking over his shoulder. Finally, he wrapped one leg around the other. He looked like a human corkscrew! But not for long. Juni's next move was to untwist himself with dizzying speed. He and his snowboard went spinning into the hooligans' midst!

"Aaaaaiiigh!" Brat cried, as Juni caught him up in his spinning vortex. The dreadlocked dude was scooped onto the spinning board for a moment, only to be tossed right off a second later. Brat landed in a heap in the snow, at which point Carmen began to ski in tight circles around him. She forcefully pushed him down every time he tried to lurch to his feet.

Juni had moved on to the next boarder, whisking him toward his father.

With the boarders distracted by this dizzying maneuver, Mom pulled herself out of the snow-bank and started whisking, too!

Before long, the four spies had scrambled their foes (those who hadn't run away, wailing in terror, that is) into submission. Juni then passed around the handcuffs. When the Cortezes headed back to the lodge, they had Brat, Clark, Reggie, and, most importantly, Manny in their custody.

Carmen and Juni led the party to the most-ignored space in the lodge—the student laundry room, of course. After cuffing each snowboarder to a coin slot on one of the neglected washers and dryers, the spies stared the hoodlums down.

"Okay," Dad announced. "By now, you may have surmised that, despite our impeccable performances, 'Signe' here is not a Swiss skiing star, and I am, believe it or not, *not* a Spanish skiing coach. Well, I *am* a Spaniard, of course. . . ."

"Uh, Dad?" Carmen prodded gently. "The point?"

"Oh, *si*," Dad harrumphed. He turned back to the boarders and declared, "We are spies. And we want answers. You have clearly spread some icy behavior amongst your fellow snowboarders, making them commit dastardly deeds. Now tell us— how did you do it?"

"Huh?" Clark blurted out.

"Dude, how do you say *indie* in Spanish?" Brat added. "'Cuz that's what we are, man. We don't recruit. In fact, we repel."

"That's obvious," Carmen said, pinching her nose as if she smelled something gross.

"Honey . . ." Mom chided her. "Just because these boarders are acting obnoxious doesn't mean we have to stoop to their level. Let's do this the OSS way, with grace and savvy."

With that, Mom marched over to stand in front of the boarders.

"You think you're *soooo* tough," she said, planting her fists on her hips and squinting at them. "Well, we'll see how tough you are after I've called . . . *your mothers!*"

Brat's bratty grin melted away. His eyes bulged with fear. Then he yelped, "No! Anything but that!"

"Har-har-har," Reggie guffawed, pointing at Brat from within his handcuffs. "What a mama's boy!"

"Oh, so *you* have nothing to fear from a call home?" Mom asked Reggie threateningly. "Even when I tell her you haven't combed your hair since you arrived, and you've been eating chocolate bars for breakfast? And that your e-mail saying you had the best McTwist at camp was a total lie?"

Reggie gulped hard. His eyes went watery.

"Please, please don't," he begged Mom. "I'll tell you anything you want to know."

"Whoa," Juni whispered to Carmen. "How'd she know all that stuff about Reggie?"

"All I'm gonna say," Carmen murmured back, "is don't *ever* play poker with Mom. She's quite the bluffer."

"All right," Mom said, giving each boarder—especially Manny—an extra-harsh stare. "Let's try this again, shall we? How have you infected all these criminals with their new, icy natures? And perhaps more important—how do we *undo* your dastardly damage?"

"Look, uh, whoever you are," Manny said, "unless these dudes have been keeping a huge secret from me—which, for the record, I would totally respect—we don't know what the heck you're talking about."

"Let's prove that, eh?" Juni said. He stepped forward and pulled a gadget out of his parka pocket. "I slipped this into my gizmo stash this morning. But I *hoped* I wouldn't have to use it."

"The Intelli-otoscope, huh?" Carmen said. "That's a good one."

"Uh . . . Intelli-*what*-oscope?" Clark said nervously.

"Don't worry, it doesn't hurt," Juni said, holding up the device—a rod topped with a pointy magnifier. It looked just like the instrument an ordinary doctor would use to peer into a patient's ear. "This'll be in one ear and out the other."

Literally!

When Juni held the instrument up to Clark's ear and pushed a button, a beam of light shot from the device. The flash burrowed into Clark's left ear and . . . emerged from his right! And *that* light beam flashed onto the wall next to Clark, just like a film projection.

Also like a movie, the beam of light was full of pictures. The first image was a pile of plastic-wrapped snack cakes. Suddenly, the cakes turned into Clark, successfully completing a 720 Spin on his snowboard. Next appeared Carmen's face, smiling sweetly!

"Ooooh," Juni hooted as Clark's thoughts continued to stream out onto the wall. "*Someone*'s got a crush."

Clark and Carmen turned bright red. Mom and Dad just smiled knowingly.

Juni's face showed his disappointment. It appeared that Clark's head really *was* empty of any information about the Moonshag crime spree.

Juni pondered over what to do next. He decided it was best to skip over Reggie and Brat and move directly on to Manny. He was the ringleader. Surely *he* knew something! When Juni approached Manny, how-ever, the dude growled and struggled against his handcuffs.

"Stay out of my head, kid," he threatened.

"Oh, so you have something to hide?" Mom piped up.

"No!"

"Well, then . . ." Juni said, stepping forward, "by orders of the OSS, we're going to take a peek."

Juni held the Intelli-otoscope up to Manny's ear. The boarder's thoughts began to dance across the wall next to him. The four Cortez spies examined the images closely.

First they saw Manny, snowboarding next to Alfredo Bomba. Bomba was, of course, on skis. Suddenly, Manny ducked in front of the portly ath-lete, tripping him and sending him tumbling down the mountain!

Next, Manny was arm-wrestling with Pokey Pleat. After a game struggle, Pokey won! But in the image, Manny smirked. He'd clearly let her win.

The kids saw that day's breakfast; Manny's child-hood sled, named Rosehips; a college term paper with a big, red C inked on top; a scampering dog; and much more.

But where was the crime-instigating formula? It

was nowhere to be found. Manny was just as ignorant as his students about the ice surging through their own veins.

The Cortezes glanced at one another, silently communicating an alarming realization: clearly, Manny and his crew were the unwitting pawns of some evildoer!

An evildoer who was still at large!

CHAPTER 11

Juni lowered the Intelli-otoscope from Manny's ear and gave his boarding buds a grave look.

"Listen, dudes," he said. "I've got some bad news for you. Your high fives have been spreading evil all over town. Everyone you touch goes icy and bad."

For a moment, the boarders gaped at Juni in stunned silence. Then Reggie's face broke into a pleased grin.

"Kewl!" he said. "We're so renegade, we've got a following."

"No!" Carmen said, stomping over to face the boarders. "Don't you understand? You've affected these people against their will. And they're not just acting obnoxious, like you dudes. They're doing really bad things. Like robbing banks!"

"And breaking ski lift cables," Juni added.

"And scaring hapless merchants to the bone," Carmen finished with a scowl.

"Dude," Clark breathed. "That's . . . bogus."

"That's the truth," Juni said, walking over to stand next to Carmen. "And somehow, you guys are at the heart of it."

"Oh, no!" Reggie cried. "Now you really *are* going to call our moms, aren't you?"

Mom and Dad glanced at each other. They exchanged a scheming wink. Years of enforcing parental discipline had prepared them for this moment.

"Boys," Dad said, waggling his thick eyebrows at the boarders. "We are prepared to make a deal with you. We will refrain from telling prosecutors *and* your mothers about your participation in these scoundrelly crimes. In exchange, you will help us."

"Help!" Manny protested. "I don't believe you understood my protégés here. We're rebels. Off the grid. We are definitely not down with the establishment. And it doesn't get any more establishment than . . . government spies."

"Hey," Juni protested. "Spying's the coolest thing ever. Do you even, like, *go* to the movies?"

"That Intelli-whatever-scope thing *was* pretty cool," Clark pointed out to Manny. "Unlike, say, naming your childhood sled Rosehips."

"Dude," Manny growled. "Don't go there."

"Oh, come on," Carmen cried, throwing up her hands. "I've *so* had it with you guys and your cool competition. Have you ever heard of getting ahead by, I don't know, being smart? Or really talented? Or, say, training hard, like Pokey Pleat?"

At this, Manny jumped.

Carmen and Juni exchanged a furtive look, while Manny tried to cover up his reaction.

"Whatever," he grumbled. "Pokey may have a medal, but she's also got all these *commitments*. Cutting ribbons at ski resorts and making ChafeStick commercials in the French Alps? *Bo-ring!*"

"*Welllll . . .*" Juni said carefully. "You are right about all of Pokey's commitments. In fact, she's agreed to help us. She's in Moonshag, tackling baddies as we speak."

"She is?" Manny and Carmen shouted at the same time.

"I mean . . ." Carmen recovered quickly. "I just didn't know she'd bagged one of the ice men so quickly. She's amazing!"

"Yes," Juni said, giving Carmen a secret wink. "I just got word of it on my spy watch."

"*That's* it," Manny shouted. "Count us in, spies. Anything Pokey can do, I can do better."

"Catchy," Juni said briskly. He stepped over to the washers and dryers and began unlocking the boarders' handcuffs. As each guy was freed, he hopped off his prisoner's perch and reached into his jacket for sustenance. Clark began popping foaming Fizzy Stones into his mouth. Brat chugged some Jitter Cola. And Manny gobbled a handful of superspicy red hots.

"Here's the deal," Mom told them as they snacked. "You are *going* to use your snowboarding skills for good, not mischief. You are going to search both the ski resort and the town for anyone with pale skin, blue lips, and bags full of loot. And you *will* make citizen's arrests, then bring the captives directly to us for processing."

"Done," Manny said, swallowing his mouthful of candy. "Under one condition."

"Oh, really?" Dad said drily. "I think you are in no position to make demands, Mr. Lass!"

But Manny pressed on.

"We will spend the day hunting down these ice dudes," Manny said, "but tonight, we've got the Ski vs. Snowboard Battle!"

"I almost forgot!" Juni cried. "Dudes, we are gonna rock!"

He held up his hand to Clark for a high five.

Then . . . he remembered that skin-to-skin contact was a no-no. *And* that the spies were supposed to be calling the shots.

"Er, I mean," Juni stuttered. "Uh, what do you think, Dad, Mom? Should we agree to Manny's condition, even though we totally don't have to?"

"That's fine," Mom said, tousling Juni's hair. "After all, if the entire freestyle team dropped out of the competition, it would certainly attract attention, wouldn't it? We want our operation to be as stealthy as possible."

"Cool!" Brat said, after gulping down another chug of Jitter Cola. "We're gonna show those skiers who's boss."

"Huh?" Dad said. "Skiers? Snowboarders? Aren't they basically the same thing?"

"What?!" the boarders roared.

"Oh, Dad," Carmen cringed. "Major faux pas. You see, the skiers and boarders have a bit of a turf war going—"

"Skiers!" Brat spat, spraying some Jitter as he did. "*Talk* about mama's boys. We're gonna really show 'em!"

"Yeah!" Reggie yelled. He was gulping down his own can of Jitter Cola. "I really *hate* those guys."

"Okay, okay, simmer down," Mom scolded the

boys. "I can understand a *little* competitive edge. Why, just last week, when I beat my husband Gregorio here in a judo showdown—"

"Ingrid!" Dad cried, looking hurt. "You promised you wouldn't tell anyone."

"See, what I mean?" Mom said with a nod. "Athletes, especially *male* ones, sometimes take winning too seriously. But it's how you play the game that cou—"

"Game?" Brat and Reggie yelled.

"Lady," Reggie said. "Boarding's no game. It's life! And the skiers are trying to encroach on our way of life, see?"

Glug, glug, glug.

Reggie paused to down some more Jitter Cola. Then he completed his thought.

"And in tonight's tournament," he yelled, "we're gonna kill 'em!"

As Mom and Juni gasped, Dad barked, "That's enough, Reggie!"

Carmen squinted at Reggie in silence.

She thought for a moment.

Then she marched up to Reggie and grabbed away his Jitter Cola. Not surprisingly, the almost-empty can was so frosty it practically burned her hand. But Carmen was a spy with a hunch.

Mere pain wouldn't deter her in her quest for intel.

Slamming the can down on top of the dusty clothes-folding table, Carmen dug into one of her parka pockets. She pulled out a small canvas carryall, unzipped it, and took out several tiny instruments: a microscope, a medicine dropper, some glass slides, and several test tubes containing chemicals.

"What's the deal?" Reggie asked, lunging toward Carmen as she set up the miniature chemistry set. "I wasn't through with that Jitter!"

"Oh, yes, you were," Juni said, moving with lightning speed to stand between Carmen and Reggie, his arms folded over his chest. "You might be the better boarder, Reg, but I've got black belts in tae kwon do, Karate, *and* Epicuriae."

"Epicuriae?" Reggie asked with a curled lip. "*What's that?*"

"*Competitive eating,*" Juni said, puffing out his belly with pride. "The dozen bowls of Fooglie Puffs I ate this morning should have clued you in. Some spy you'd make."

"Quiet!" Carmen ordered from her spot behind the bickering boarders. She'd just donned a white lab coat and a pair of protective goggles that made her brown eyes look huge and buggy.

"I need to concentrate," she continued. "This analysis is going to be very delicate. While I'm at it, hand over some of those red hots and Fizzy Stones. I want to get a load of everything you guys have been noshing on."

The spies and boarders hovered breathlessly nearby as Carmen used a medicine dropper to dispense the drink and candy samples into several small test tubes. To each tube, she added a different combination of chemicals. She looked around the filthy laundry room in disgust.

"What I wouldn't give for a decent agitator and an autoclave," she said.

Since those weren't handy, she thrust a couple of the test tubes into the hands of Clark and Brat.

"Shake those until I say you can stop," she directed them. Stunned into submission, the boys began shaking the test tubes.

Next, Carmen jerry-rigged one of the washing machines to wash the remaining tubes in a bath of boiling water.

In precisely five minutes, the samples were ready. Carmen dribbled the solutions onto several slides and placed the slides beneath the microscope. She began murmuring to herself.

"Mm-hmmmm," she whispered. "Yes, yes. Very

interesting. Oh, and check out that dual-bond binary peptide! Fascinating."

"Oh, for crying out loud," Juni finally said in exasperation. "Would you cut the Madame Curie act and tell us what the heck you're doing?"

Carmen held up one finger.

"There's one more thing I need to check. . . ." she said as she began typing into her spy watch. "Just to confirm my suspicion, I'm looking at the OSS's online index of D.C.s."

"D.C.s?" Manny whispered to Mom as Carmen typed away.

"Dastardly chemicals," Mom explained.

Carmen looked up from her watch with a grin.

"Just as I thought!" she announced. "That junk food is spiked! It's full of ACY Serum!"

"You're kidding!" Juni, Mom, and Dad cried. To the boarders' blank stares, Juni quickly explained, "ACY, of course, stands for 'Aorta Chill You'! The stuff turns your veins to ice and hardens your heart. Then it lodges in your sweat glands."

"That must be why you guys were able to pass on the syndrome through your high fives," Carmen said. "Sweaty palms."

"Sweat, preferably stinky sweat, *is* a hallmark of

every snowboarder worth his salt," Clark admitted with a shrug.

"So, we were drugged through our eats?" Brat asked. "Dude, that's completely creepy! But also kinda brilliant! I mean, snackage and snowboarding are our only reasons for living."

"Who's behind this?" Carmen wondered. Turning to all four boarders, she demanded, "Where did you get this grub?"

Nervously, Clark glanced at Manny, then looked away. Brat, too, peeked at the instructor. Finally, Reggie broke down and pointed at Manny, crying, "He gave us a whole stash of it!"

The spies stared at Manny suspiciously.

"Is that true, Lass?" Dad demanded.

"Yeah," he admitted, a bit sheepishly. "Listen, stolen munchies taste a lot better than grub that's been bought from the Brockenhip snack bar. So . . . I might have filched this stuff from the faculty après-ski den."

"Après-ski den, eh?" Dad said.

"*Tscha*," Manny said. "It's located in a tower on top of the lodge. Killer view. All the instructors hang out there après-ski—after skiing. *Except* yours truly, of course. That place is all about elevator music and dignified conversation. Lame!"

"But their, eh, how you say, *snackage* was good enough for you?" Dad growled.

"Well . . . yeah," Manny said. "In fact, I'm the only one who was interested in this stuff. The other teachers prefer hoity-toity stuff like wine and cheese. And you know, Pokey. She's the original granola girl. None of them are interested in neon-green snack cakes and gummy worms and stuff like that."

"How . . . convenient," Carmen said, raising her eyebrows. Then she turned to her spy family.

"I could use a little R & R," she said sneakily. "Why don't we visit this secret après-ski den?"

"Sure," Mom said, returning her daughter's mischievous grin. "I wouldn't mind a little wine and cheese to go with . . . my *spying*."

CHAPTER 12

Together, the spies and the snowboarders left the laundry room. The boarders grinned at their new handlers, then headed out the lodge door to scour Moonshag for icy villains.

And the Cortezes headed for the après-ski den.

To keep meddlesome junior athletes away from the adults-only atelier, Alfredo Bomba had constructed the den in the most remote turret of the giant lodge. He'd also booby-trapped the corridors that led to the place.

Luckily, Manny knew the route cold—so to speak—and had drawn the Cortezes a map before he set out for town.

Now Dad peered at the map and led his family to a broom closet off the lodge's main lobby. He burrowed into the messy closet looking for a spigot in the wall. He turned the faucet handle two twists to the right, and three to the left.

With a low rumble, the closet's back wall sank

into the floor, revealing a narrow, dark stairwell.

"Whoa!" Carmen breathed as the spies began to ascend the steps. "Bomba sure likes his privacy, doesn't he? I wonder what kind of crazy stuff he's got in this après-ski den?"

"We'll find out soon!" Dad said with determination.

Swiftly, the spies climbed up, up, up the stairs. When the stairwell finally ended, they found themselves facing both a ladder and a slide. Mom, Carmen, and Juni headed for the ladder.

"Ah, ah, ah," Dad admonished them, pointing at the map. "We'll take the chute."

"But isn't the turret on *top* of the lodge?" Carmen protested. "That makes no sense."

"I agree," Dad said. "But that's what Manny told us to do. . . ."

As he said this, Dad's face became thoughtful, then stony.

"Dad," Carmen said quietly. "You don't think Manny lied to us, do you?"

"If he did," Mom said, "then we've got our villain."

"Juni knows Manny best," Dad said. "We will do what he says."

Mom, Dad, and Carmen gazed at the youngest Cortez. Juni felt sweat break out on his upper lip.

He pulled nervously at his fleece collar. Then, he began to think hard about Manny Lass. He mused on the subject of Manny's renegade philosophy and surly independence. He pictured the dogged dedication Manny threw into his McTwists and 360 Spins.

Next, Juni contemplated the things in Manny's innermost thoughts—Pokey Pleat and Rosehips, the sled.

Finally, Juni nodded. After the incident with the Intelli-otoscope, he was *sure* there was more to Manny than attitude and anger.

"We'll take the slide," he announced to his family.

Nodding in agreement, Dad hopped into the slick chute. Instantly, he disappeared.

"Aaaaaaagh!" Dad's terrified screams echoed back to his family.

Exchanging apprehensive looks, the spies took deep breaths. They all shrugged. What choice did they have?

Mom mounted the slide and swooped away, shrieking, *"Whooooaaa!"*

Then it was Juni's turn: *"Aiiiiggggh!"*

Finally, Carmen gritted her teeth and plunged into the slide.

"Bwaaaaaah!" she screamed. She found herself

somersaulting and spinning down the twisty-turny slide. The chute veered and plunged and angled violently. Luckily, just when Carmen thought she could take no more, it ended. Unfortunately, though, it ended in midair! Just behind the rest of her family, Carmen found herself falling through a long, narrow chamber! She squeezed her eyes shut and braced for pain.

Sproing! Boing! Sproing! Boing!

What luck, again! Instead of splatting onto a hard floor, the spies found themselves bouncing off a trampoline that had been stretched across the bottom of the tower. The powerful rebounds sent them soaring into the upper reaches of the dusky, log-lined tower. As Dad reached the crest of his bounce, he spotted a narrow ledge jutting out from one of the tower's walls. He lunged for it and caught it!

"Over here!" he called to his family as they soared upward.

Soon, all four Cortezes were dangling from the narrow ledge. With their spy-honed agility, they flipped themselves up on top of it. Now, they were facing an ornate door.

Dad looked at Manny's map, sweat-stained and crumpled in his fist.

"This is it!" he said. "It had better be worth it!"

Assuming the arrogant expressions of Signe Schuss and Don Coyote, Mom and Dad marched through the door. Since children were barred from the den, Carmen and Juni kept themselves hidden. Carmen spied on the scene through the peephole, Juni through the keyhole.

As they checked out the après-ski den, all four spies had to stifle gasps. The place was incredible. Floor-to-ceiling windows in every wall framed incredible mountain views. In the center of the high-ceilinged room, ski instructors in bathing suits gamboled in a frothy hot tub. At a sumptuous bar, a man in a bow tie was serving up warm, mulled wine and toasted bread and cheese. In a far corner of the room, some instructors were laughing as they played a spirited game of bingo. And in another, Pokey Pleat was stretching in a fully outfitted Pilates zone.

"Whoa," Juni breathed to his sister. "The grown-ups were holding out on us. This place is as posh as it gets."

"And look who's in the middle of it all, lapping up the luxury," Carmen noted. "Alfredo Bomba. Retired ski stars sure are greedy!"

Carmen wasn't kidding. Bomba was lounging in an extra-squashy recliner. At one of his elbows was a tray laden with wine, as well as cheese, peeled grapes, and a crusty loaf of bread. At his other elbow was a manicurist, smiling sweetly as she buffed Bomba's nails to a shine.

When he spotted Mom and Dad, Bomba paused in his luxuriating. He regarded the spies with suspicious, beady eyes. Carmen and Juni held their breath.

Soon it became clear that the secret identities of Mom and Dad were still secure. Bomba's shiny face broke into a wide grin.

"Ah," he called. "We have surprise visitors! A rarity in the oh-so-exclusive après-ski den. You must be the famous Signe Schuss and Don Coyote. I heard you were visiting Brockenhip. I'm very honored that you could join us."

Dad hesitated before he said, "Well, one of the skiers on the slopes clued me in." He made his way toward Bomba with his hand extended for a friendly shake. "And I thought—only the best for my world-class skier, Signe. You understand, eh?"

"Of course, of course, Señor Coyote," Bomba said. "Please, help yourselves to some snacks."

"Well, thank you," Mom said in her thick, imitation-Swiss accent. She popped a grape into her mouth and smiled gratefully.

"I must say, Señor Bomba," she continued in a loud voice. "It is refreshing to receive such gracious treatment. I feel I have been absolutely battered by those unwelcoming snowboarders! They have been so rude!"

Mom looked around the après-ski den for nods of agreement. Many of the ski instructors gave them. Some of the snowboarding teachers merely shrugged and grinned, as if to say, "What are you gonna do?"

Only Pokey Pleat spoke out.

"Hey, don't paint all us boarders with that brush," she protested, gazing across the den at Mom. As she spoke, she folded her muscled legs into a lotus position and took a bite out of a carrot. "Some of us are serious athletes, y'know. We don't have time to bother with terrorizing skiers on the slopes."

"As your boarders like to say, Pokey," Bomba said, rolling his eyes. "*What*-ever!"

Then the skier turned back to Mom.

"I'm so sorry if these ruffians have sullied your stay here at Brockenhip," he said. "They *are* horrid, aren't they? Have you heard about this crime spree in town? I'm certain the culprits are all boarders. Renegades on the slopes, rebels in life, I always say."

"*Si*, it is terrible, isn't it?" Dad agreed. "First, those snowboarders take over our noble sport—skiing. Then they commandeer your town. They are ruining things for everyone!"

"Well . . . just about everyone," Bomba said cryptically. "And that's not all! They're getting worse! Every new batch of boarders that arrives at our program seems more rebellious than the last. I fear for our way of life! *Tsk, tsk!*"

"Bomba!" Pokey cried, leaping to her feet. She was so mad, she'd abandoned her stretches. Pokey was even ignoring her healthy snack.

"She's seriously enraged," Carmen whispered to Juni. "Do you think maybe she—"

"—Has something to hide?" Juni finished. "Looks that way. We'd better keep an eye on her!"

The kids returned their attention to the boarder, whose blond braids were trembling with anger.

"I've had enough of your dissing us," Pokey hissed to Bomba. "Not *all* boarders are packing rude 'tude. Some of us just want to enjoy the mountains, like you skiers. Some of us want snowboarding to become a legitimate sport—one with pride and history and, yes, gold medals. And I'm not going to let *you* stomp all over that dream, old man."

Mom, Dad, Bomba, and several other instructors around the room blinked at Pokey in surprise. A few of them seemed moved. Others yawned exaggeratedly. But only Mom took action—a surprising one! She turned her back on Pokey, totally dissing her. Then, her voice dripping with fake delight, she cried, "Oh, look at that!" She pointed to a snack station near the door where Carmen and Juni were hidden. As Mom strode over to the snack bar, Pokey huffed in frustration and stomped back to her workout mat. Carmen could almost hear the boarder's angry thoughts: I should have known not to pour my heart out to a bunch of posh, shallow skiers!

For a moment, Carmen felt a stab of sympathy for Pokey. Maybe what she'd said was true. Maybe all boarders *weren't* bad.

And maybe skiers *were* a little arrogant.

Carmen was tempted to delve into some deep thoughts about underdogs and top dogs and class warfare and such. But she didn't have that luxury. Mom was about to close in on the truth, or at least the snacks! Carmen had to be on her toes.

As the Spy Girl returned her attention to the après-ski den, Mom reached the snack station. She winked at Carmen and Juni's door. Then she pulled a shiny foil packet off the station's shelf.

"Oooh!" she exclaimed loudly. "Fizzy Stones! My favorite candy. I love the way they explode in your mouth. Especially when you mix them with . . . Jitter Cola!"

With great enthusiasm, Mom grabbed a hot-pink can of Jitter Cola out of a small fridge next to the snack stand. Juni covered his mouth to suppress a giggle. In real life, Mom wouldn't have come within ten feet of such a junky refreshment.

And it seemed Alfredo Bomba felt the same way. The moment Mom started to tear open the pouch of Fizzy Stones, he shoved his manicurist out of the way and leapt from his recliner.

"Signe, Signe," he protested, hurrying over to Mom. "Those are silly snowboarders' snacks. Wouldn't you prefer some cognac instead? And we have some nice cheese aging in our wine cellar. It's extra moldy, just the way most grown-ups like it."

"Well, I *do* like moldy cheese," Mom admitted. "But I also love Jitter Cola. Why do you protest, Bomba? Is something wrong with these snacks?"

"Not if you like hyperactivity and obnoxious behavior," Bomba replied with a sniff.

Dad appeared at Bomba's and Mom's sides.

"Obnoxious behavior," he said. "That would be completely out of character for a . . . skier, eh?"

"You read my mind," Bomba said, nodding smugly.

There's our cue, Carmen thought. Grabbing Juni, she suddenly kicked open their door and burst into the après-ski den. She pointed at the stunned ski director and said, "Funny you should mention mind reading, Mr. Bomba. Because we happen to have an Intelli-otoscope right here. And you know what I bet we'd find if we used it to peer into your head?"

"What?!" Bomba sputtered.

"I think we'd discover a man who's been pinning a bad rap on snowboarders, then drugging them with ACY Serum so they'll commit crimes on his behalf," Carmen said accusingly. "The boarders get all the blame and you, Mr. Bomba, get off scot-free. Well, the jig is up, dude. You're under arrest!"

Juni gazed at his sister in awe.

"Cool speech," he admitted. "You totally defended the boarders' honor."

Carmen grinned at her brother before whipping a set of handcuffs out from beneath her ski parka. With Juni at her side, she approached Bomba in order to take him into custody.

But Bomba had other ideas. With a fleetness one would never have expected from the portly retiree, Bomba whipped some handcuffs out of his own ski suit. He slapped the cuffs onto Mom and yanked her over to a gear rack near the bar. Grabbing a handful of bungee cords, Bomba strapped Mom onto his back as if she were a long-legged papoose. Mom kicked and struggled and grunted in protest, but she was powerless to escape.

Now Bomba began lumbering toward one of the den's big windows. As he went, he pulled something else from his ski suit—a small remote-control device.

"Stop!" Dad commanded the criminal.

Bomba, of course, did not stop. Instead, he pushed a button on the device. The window opened with an electronic hum.

Bomba hit another button.

Long skis suddenly sprouted from his boots. He'd had an escape plan all prepared!

The next thing the Spy Kids knew, Bomba leapt through the window and began skimming down the mountain. In seconds, he—and Mom—had disappeared!

CHAPTER 13

Immediately, the Spy Kids and their dad sprang into action.

"Dude!" Juni exclaimed. "We've so got our work cut out for us. We've got to apprehend our villain— Bomba—and rescue Mom. *Then* we have to figure out how to reverse the ACY Serum and de-freeze all the boarding baddies."

"And while we're at it," Carmen added breathlessly, "we might want to try to redeem the sport of snowboarding. I've got to admit, boarders don't *totally* deserve their bad rap."

"Gee, thanks," Pokey said drily. She loped up to Bomba's open escape window and gazed after the swiftly departing villain. Behind her, other instructors were murmuring amongst themselves in alarm.

"I guess," Pokey added, glancing over her shoulder at Carmen, "it took a psycho skier to talk some sense into you."

Carmen shot Pokey a glare. But she didn't have

time to bicker with the sulky boarder. She was on a mission! She turned to Juni and Dad.

"So, which item do we tackle first?" she asked them.

"Mom, of course," Juni cried.

"*Si, si,*" Dad growled, glaring out the window. "Quick, children—a strategy!"

"Uh, chase after 'em?" Juni proposed.

"*Excellent* strategy," Dad roared. "Grab your board, Juni! Carmen and I will ski."

The spies raced to the gear rack and grabbed boards and skis. As Carmen began to click her boots into her skis, Pokey turned away from the open window.

"Dude," she said to Carmen. "Unless you're some sort of Euro-prodigy, you're never gonna catch Bomba on skis. The guy was born with blades in the soles of his feet. Even if he is old and chubby, he's still the best skier that ever was."

"Uh-huh," Carmen said, rolling her eyes. She started to clomp toward the open window, dragging along the skis she'd chosen. But Pokey intercepted her, planting her fists on her hips and shaking her head.

"Girlfriend," she insisted. "You need to grab a snowboard."

"Last I checked, *you* were the best snowboarder that ever was," Carmen snapped at Pokey. "So, maybe *you* need to grab a board and help us— instead of just sitting on your butt and dispensing your indie advice."

Pokey's freckled face grew dark. Her eyebrows met in a blond *V*. Her ChafeSticked lips tightened into a thin line.

Many of the boarding instructors in the room gasped.

"Ooooh!" one of them stage-whispered. "Pokey is *P.O.*'d!"

Pokey stared Carmen down.

"Those are challenging words," she growled at the young spy.

"You bet they are," Carmen declared.

At that, Pokey . . . grinned!

"Kid," she declared. "I like you! Let's hit it!"

Pokey marched to the gear rack and grabbed herself a board. She tossed additional snowboards to Dad and Carmen. Within seconds, the three spies and the Olympic star were careening down the mountain, schussing madly toward their prey.

"Whoooaaaaa!" Dad said, wobbling wildly on his snowboard as he hurtled down the hill. "How do you steer this thing?"

Juni was about to give his father some quick instructions when, out of the corner of his eye, he noticed Carmen. She was crouching low on her board, leaning into her edges with supreme confidence, and spraying snow like a pro.

Clearly, Juni wasn't the only natural in the Cortez clan!

"Watch *her*!" Juni told Dad, pointing at his snow-skimming sister.

Dad grinned and gave Juni a thumbs-up. Then Juni shot ahead and joined Carmen and Pokey. They whizzed down the mountain, barely digging into the snow to slow themselves. They had to save Mom!

It wasn't long before they spotted Bomba below them, with Mom still strapped to his back. Even with his human cargo, Carmen realized, the man skied like a dream.

"Just look at that, folks! The man skis like a dream!"

Carmen jumped and looked around. How had her thought just been broadcast into the wintry air?! And by the cheery voice of a grown man, for that matter?

Only when Carmen heard a burst of applause and more chatter from the booming voice did she understand what was happening.

Our chase has just blundered into the middle of the Ski vs. Snowboard Battle! she thought. On national TV! *Aarghh!*

"Well, this *is* a pleasant surprise for our spectators," the announcer was saying. "Not to mention our KCN viewers at home. Looks like we're being treated to an exhibition by the legendary Alfredo Bomba and . . . an unidentified woman strapped to his back! Perhaps this is a new Olympic event in the making. Piggy-skiing, perhaps? Or synchronized-blade ballet?"

As the announcer nattered on, Carmen slapped her forehead with her mittened hand.

Way to be undercover, she scolded herself. How're we going to make this look intentional?

Before she could devise a plan, she was distracted by a new wave of cheers. Looking for the source, she saw that Bomba had slowed his sprint down the mountain. In fact, he'd begun hotdogging around the ski run, jerking Mom this way and that.

With each fancy move, the audience roared with approval.

"Bomba is totally lapping up the adulation," Carmen muttered angrily. "Even as he's in the middle of a kidnapping and crime spree. Talk about vain!"

Carmen shook her head in disgust. Which turned out to be a grave mistake, given the fact that she was a snowboarding newbie. Suddenly, she lost her balance. Her board swooped out from under her!

"Whoaaaaaa!" Carmen screamed as she hurtled into a crazy spin. Her vision blurred. Her lungs lurched. She got so dizzy she thought she was going to hurl her oatmeal!

But, somehow, she righted herself. And she was rewarded by a roar of approval from the crowd, as well as a nod from the KCN announcer.

"Hold the phone!" the announcer burbled. "Bomba isn't the only showboat on our slope! We've just witnessed a brilliant combination of freestyle and downhill boarding by a junior ski student! Who *is* that mystery girl?"

A whispering sound filled the chill air. A moment later, the announcer said, "Well, we've just learned her identity. She's a skiing student who's turned to the board, folks. Welcome to your new sport, Miss Carmen Cortez!"

"Yayyyyyy!" the crowd cheered.

Carmen cringed.

Okay, she scolded herself under her breath. It doesn't *get* less undercover than that. Real cool, Cortez.

When Carmen noticed something at the bottom of the mountain, she realized she might actually *have* pulled a smooth move.

That something was Alfredo Bomba, skidding to a halt and glaring up the mountain. Carmen had stolen his thunder, and he was so enraged he seemed to have forgotten that he was running from the law!

"Well, I'll remind him," Carmen growled out loud.

She turned to Juni, Pokey, and Dad and yelled, "The more the crowd loves us, the more Bomba hates us. So you know what to do!"

"No problemo!" Juni hooted. He immediately launched into a series of star moves. He waved to the crowd and grinned goofily. He launched himself into a showy Misty Flip.

The audience responded with wild cheers.

So, Carmen and Pokey fed them more entertainment. They linked hands and spun each other in a wild gyration.

The crowd roared with laughter. Next, Carmen and Pokey wiggled their hips sassily, setting off another round of adoration from the crowd.

That was when Alfredo Bomba cut in. He stomped his ski, puffed out his belly and threw a star-sized hissy fit.

"Arresto!" he screamed. "You dare to root for these snowboarding brats over the great Bomba? What kind of cretins are you?"

Suddenly, the crowd went silent. After a stunned pause, a lone voice in the crowd shouted, "Bogus, dude!"

"Booooo!" called another.

Soon the air was filled with boos and hisses. Bomba's shoulders began to sag. His stocky legs got weak. He hung his head in disgrace.

That was the only opening the spies needed. The moment Bomba let down his guard, they swooped down upon him like a flash blizzard. Before the mad skier could react, Juni had reached for a crucial nerve behind his knee, temporarily immobilizing the man. Carmen cut away Mom's bindings with her acid crayon. Finally, Dad swept Mom up in a big, celebratory kiss.

"Ewww!" Juni cried, releasing Bomba's knee to recoil in horror. "Could you *please* refrain from mushy stuff in front of your children?!"

"Not to mention," Carmen added, "the million or so people watching on KCN. Oh, the humiliation!"

"Uh, speaking of humiliation," Mom said, pulling away from Dad so she could point at

Bomba in alarm. "Our captive is getting away!"

She was right! When Juni had released Bomba's knee to reprimand his racy 'rents, the villain had slithered out of the spies' reach. By the time any of the Cortezes realized what was happening, Bomba had begun skimming down the hill.

Now he was hundreds of yards ahead of them and getting faster all the time!

"Noooooo!" Juni cried. "This is all my fault."

"We'll point fingers later," Carmen said to her brother. "Right now, we've got to re-snag that skier! But how? He's lightning-fast, especially now that he's unloaded Mom!"

Juni gaped blankly at the crowd—at all the expectant faces waiting for him to save the day.

He looked at his panicked family, feeling guilt suffuse every part of his body.

Then he ripped open his parka and scanned his gizmo-packed ski vest, searching desperately for a solution.

Oh, man, Juni wailed inwardly. Where's a good whoopee cushion when you . . . need . . . one?

Juni's thought trailed off as his eye fell upon a brick-sized gizmo tucked into one of his pockets. It was red and shiny and covered with hinges and seams. It was perfect!

Juni's face broke into a giddy grin. He gazed at his family and announced: "You want a solution? Well, I've got one word for you!"

He threw back his head and sang, "Bob-a-Luuuuuggge!"

CHAPTER 14

Within thirty seconds, Juni had unfolded Uncle Machete's collapsible bobsled/luge hybrid and planted its superslick blades into the snow. He shot his family and Pokey a rakish wink and said, "Even Bomba can't outrun this baby! Call the OSS helicopters and tell 'em we're making a take-out order!"

"Enough with the quips," Carmen said, though she couldn't help grinning. "Go!"

Juni went! As he pushed off down the ski run, then jumped onto the Bob-a-Luuuge, he heard the KCN announcer's voice echoing after him: "And *what* a surprising finish to the Ski vs. Snowboard Battle, ladies and gents. A synchronized-board performance, a tantrum by the great Alfredo Bomba, and some sort of bizarro sled! What won't they think of next? More importantly, what will our judges think? Stay tuned. Our winners will be announced in only a few minutes!"

An image of himself ascending a podium for some big boarding medal flashed through Juni's head. But he shook the thought away.

"You're a spy," he muttered to himself. "It's time to put mission before glory."

The thought filled Juni with determination. He hunched low in his Bob-a-Luuuge. The air whistled past his ears. His hair flapped in the wind. And finally, in Juni's blurred line of vision, Alfredo Bomba appeared!

A moment later, Bomba's already sizable butt began growing bigger and bigger. Juni was gaining on him.

The Spy Boy threw back his head and cackled in triumph. But when he refocused himself on his quest, he gasped.

He wasn't bearing down on Bomba anymore. He was facing a phalanx of surly dudes in fleece! In the moment Juni had glanced away, a small army of snowboarders had suddenly crowded onto the ski run. Now they lined up across it horizontally. They'd formed a human blockade between Juni and Bomba.

Each boarder was scowling. And white-faced. And blue-lipped.

They've been infected by ACY Serum, Juni realized. And now they're out to make my mission impossible! Noooooo!

Juni slammed on the Bob-a-Luuuge's brakes and skidded to a shuddery halt, just before crashing into one of the snowboarders. He looked up at the dude and cleared his throat.

"By orders of the OSS . . ." he piped up, wishing his ten-year-old voice were a bit less squeaky, "get out of my way. I've got to catch Alfredo Bomba. He's a criminal mastermind."

"Out of your way?" one of the pale teenagers drawled. "Is that any way to talk to the dudes who want to help you out? We're after Bomba, too."

"The big blowhard," one of the other boarders added.

Juni blinked in surprise. Then he grinned and said, "Thanks, dudes! The more, the merrier."

"Kewl," the first boarder said. He held up a snow-covered hand for a high five. "Put 'er there, partner!"

"Uh . . . no thanks," Juni said, coming up with a hasty excuse. "Uh, no time. Criminals to catch and all."

"Right," the dude said. "Okay, then. Let's go!"

Together, the snowboarders and Bob-a-Luuuger tore after Bomba. With their collective speed and cunning, they caught up to him in no time. Juni shot in front of the skier and skidded, blocking Bomba's path. When the villain stopped and spun around to flee, he found himself facing a tight circle of boarders.

He was caught!

"Halt!" Juni cried, jumping out of his vehicle and hurrying toward the bewildered Bomba. "I'm placing you under arrest."

"Oh, no, you're not," said a drawling teenage voice behind Juni. Confused, the Spy Boy spun around to face one of his new boarder buds. The dude was leering at Juni mischievously.

"Oh, no! You're in cahoots with Bomba, aren't you?" Juni cried. "You're double-crossing me."

"Not even, dude," the boy scoffed. "We're in cahoots with no one. We're ind—"

"Indie, indie, I know." Juni sighed. "Then, what do you mean, I can't arrest Bomba?"

"I just meant," the lanky boarder said, taking another step toward Juni and the old skier, "that we're not going to let you take Bomba away . . . until we've had some fun with him."

"Huh?" Juni said.

The boarders didn't answer him. They simply cried out, "Get Bomba!"

One of them scooped up a handful of snow and pelted Bomba with it. The skier screamed and covered his head. The gang laughed.

They began hitting Bomba with more snow. And then sticks. And even stones. The man was terrified. And Juni wasn't feeling so good himself.

Ducking to avoid being pelted by the snowballs meant for Bomba, Juni yelled, "Stop it! Bomba may be a villain, but that's no excuse for torturing him. The OSS doesn't treat its captives this way."

The snowboarders paused for a moment. They gazed at Juni thoughtfully. Then one of them got a sneaky look on his sheet-white face and yelled, "Wedgie!"

"Wedgie! Wedgie! Wedgie!" the other boarders echoed. In an instant, they'd all lunged toward Juni with evil glints in their eyes. They were going to follow through on their threat.

Trembling with fear, Juni reached for the walkie-talkie button on his spy watch.

"Carmen," he croaked. "Help!"

From the sidelines of the ski slope further up the mountain, Mom, Dad, and Carmen had been watching in horror as the boarders began their onslaught. So, by the time Juni called with his SOS, his family was already discussing strategy.

"We can't beat them up," Mom fretted. "After all, those are innocent boys under the influence of Bomba's evil serum."

"The only way to stop them," Dad agreed, "is with an ACY antidote."

"Gotcha!" Carmen said. She began typing madly into her spy watch's computer. Booting up its wireless Internet connection, she hacked into the OSS's antidote database. But once she was in the system, she was horrified to find absolutely no intel on ACY Serum.

Frantically, Carmen searched other, top-secret antidote Web sites. But each search came up dry.

"Uh, scratch that 'gotcha,'" Carmen finally wailed. "I can't find an antidote anywhere."

"What a bummer, dude."

Carmen jumped and turned around. It was Pokey who'd spoken. She was stretching out on the snow nearby, munching a post-chase granola bar.

"Lemme know if there's anything I can do," Pokey offered, with a somewhat sheepish smile.

Carmen squinted at Pokey's granola bar.

She took in the boarder's rosy cheeks and pouty lips, her sparkling eyes and her shiny, yellow hair.

Hmmm, Carmen thought. Then, on impulse, she darted over to Pokey and grabbed the granola bar out of the boarder's hand.

"Hey," Pokey said. "Watch the snackage, girl-friend! If you want your own, you just have to ask. I've got a whole stash in my parka."

Pokey dug an assortment of crunchy, whole-some snacks from her pockets.

"Here," she offered. "I've got gorp, apples, wheat-germ packets—the whole nine."

"I'll take 'em all!" Carmen said, swiping the booty from Pokey's arms. The boarder, not to men-tion Mom and Dad, looked completely bewildered. But Carmen didn't have time to explain. Sticking the snacks into her own pockets, she pushed off on her snowboard. As she began to whiz toward Juni, Bomba, and the snowball-beaming boarders, she was jolted by the voice of the KCN announcer. She'd almost forgotten that this mission was taking place under the eyes of countless spectators and TV viewers.

"Carmen Cortez!" the announcer shrilled, star-tling Carmen even more. "Where are you going? The judges have just announced their decision, and *you*'ve won the downhill boarding title. You've trounced the skiers, girlfriend. Way to go! We need you on the podium in five."

Carmen waved gratefully at the judges, but kept on going. She had to think of her mission before glory, after all.

The crowd roared in approval.

"That's the indie spirit," the announcer cried.

"Whatever," Carmen muttered. She smiled at the crowd politely before continuing down the mountain.

Seconds later, she arrived at the cluster of boarders. She broke into their midst, sending several of the dudes sprawling.

With the boarders distracted, the sobbing Bomba began to crawl away. But Carmen snarled at him threateningly, stopping him in his tracks.

From the sidelines, Juni stared at his sister. Talk about attitude!

"Uh, Carmen?" Juni asked gently. "You . . . haven't been high-fiving anyone, have you?"

Carmen answered Juni with a wink that silently said, "I'm undercover. Work with me, here!"

Juni winked back. He watched to see what Carmen would do next.

She turned to the boarders and said, "So you showed Bomba who's boss. Nice job, dudes. And I've got your reward. Food!"

Carmen tossed each boarder some of Pokey's crunchy grub. Eagerly, the boarders swiped the snacks out of the air. But when they took a closer look at their booty—which ranged from apples and carrots to trail mix and wheatgrass juice—they groaned.

"Dude," one of them protested. "This stuff is, like, healthy!"

"It's also hot!" Carmen added with a grin. "I stole it from the faculty lounge, dudes. 'Cuz we all know that swiped snackage tastes better than gainfully gotten gorp."

"Girlfriend's got a point," one of the boarders said sagely. He took a loud bite out of an apple and crunched it with his mouth open.

"Hey," he exclaimed a moment later. "Kinda tasty! Who knew an actual apple could taste as good as, say, Sour Apple Wacky Taffy?"

As the boy spoke, Juni blinked at him in shock. The snowboarder's cheeks were turning pink! And his lips were reddening.

As the other dudes began to munch on their healthy snacks, they, too, began to exude healthy glows.

They also started smiling.

They stopped slouching and dropped their sticks and snowballs. One of them even congratulated Carmen on her snowboarding medal!

They'd undergone a total 'tude turnaround!

"What—?" Juni started to asked Carmen.

"De-fiber-illator!" Carmen whispered with a grin. "It's probably been years since these guys have experienced snackage that wasn't deep-fried, tie-dyed, or high-fructosed. The healthy food is such a shock to their systems that their hearts are warming up, and the ACY Serum is being leached out of their pores."

"Nice work," Juni exclaimed. He held his palm up in the air. "Put 'er there!"

"No prob," Carmen grinned, slapping Juni with a high five.

Schussss! Schussss! Schussss!

Suddenly the Spy Kids were surrounded by a bunch of *other* celebrators, from Pokey Pleat to Mom and Dad to Manny, Clark, Brat, and Juni's other boarding buds.

Mom and Dad gave their Spy Kids congratulatory hugs. Then they cuffed Alfredo Bomba and led him to the OSS helicopter that had just chirruped onto the ski slope.

Carmen and Juni fielded a flurry of high fives, celebratory hoots, and congratulatory hugs from the fleece-clad boarders.

"Y'know, dude," Brat said to Juni. "I think I learned something from this whole episode. Being indie is cool and all, but saving the world is even cooler."

Just so his buds wouldn't think he was *too* much of a goody-goody, though, Brat capped the thought off with a loud burp. Everybody laughed appreciatively. Everybody, that is, except Manny. He was walking over to Pokey Pleat.

"Y'know," he said when he alighted before her, "I've gotta second Brat's emotion. Not the burp. The thing he said about, y'know, being so indie."

"Oh, yeah?" Pokey drawled with a small smile.

"Yeah," Manny said with a shrug. "I mean, the indie life can get lonely. What I mean by that is, Pokey, will you have dinner with me tonight?"

All reveling ceased as the boarders, the Spy Kids, even the departing Alfredo Bomba gaped at Manny Lass.

"Romance budding between a freestyler and a downhiller?" Dad noted. "That sounds like a marriage between two battling spies. Which is to say, a match made in heaven."

"Oh, Gregorio," Mom said, smiling coyly at her husband as she hauled Bomba into the OSS helicopter.

"Oh, Ingrid," Dad said, blowing his wife a kiss.

"Oh, no, you don't!" Juni yelled.

"Yeah," Carmen agreed. "Can we get through one mission without mushy stuff? Honestly."

"You're right," Mom said, turning away from Dad with a grin. "After all, who has time for mushy stuff when there's snowboarding *and* skiing to enjoy? C'mon, kids. We've got a whole afternoon before we head back to our sun-drenched homeland. Let's hit the slopes!"